SCORPIONS

SCOR

PIONS

BY WALTER DEAN MYERS

Published by
The Trumpet Club
666 Fifth Avenue
New York, New York 10103

ISBN: 0-440-84083-X

Reprinted by arrangement with Harper & Row, Publishers
Printed in the United States of America
September 1989

10 9 8 7 6 5 4 3 2 1
OPM

To Brandon, Brian, Beverly

SCORPIONS

CHAPTER ONE

"You see anything?"

"No."

"Why don't you go down to the subway?"

"Suppose she come on the bus or take a taxi?"

"She ain't got the money for no taxi."

"She could still take the bus."

Jamal sat in the window and looked down the street. It had rained earlier, and he wondered if his mother had taken an umbrella.

"I'm hungry," Sassy said.

"You ate." Jamal answered his little sister without looking at her.

"You want to watch television?"

"You the one who always want to watch it," Jamal said.

"I just asked," Sassy said. "You worried?"

"Ain't nothing to be worried about."

"Then how come you sitting at the window ever since six o'clock?"

"How come you ask so many questions?"

"I'm gonna tell Mama you being nasty to me."

"Tell her."

"I'm gonna tell her you said that, too."

"I don't care."

"I'm putting the television on," Sassy said.

Jamal glanced at the clock on the wall. It was almost ten thirty. He started to ask Sassy if she had finished her homework, then changed his mind. He looked down into the street again.

At the corner a thin man leaned against the light pole. Jamal watched as the man leaned slowly toward the ground, then straightened up. Jamal knew that the addict would repeat his nodding until he fell asleep. He looked away.

Sassy was watching some stupid program. The television was okay, even if the programs were stupid. When he got a job, he was going to buy one of those recording machines. Then he and Mama could go and get movies and watch them instead of all the stupid stuff they had on regular television.

He thought about how he would tell Mama he had the money for the recording machine. Maybe he wouldn't even tell her—just go out and buy it for her and bring it on in the house.

Sassy fell asleep on the couch at eleven o'clock.

He moved away from the window and sat next to his sister. Mama would say that he should wake her and tell her to go to bed, but he didn't want to sit by himself.

Somebody had a radio on. Probably Snookie. Snookie always played his radio too loud. Jamal had told Snookie about his loud playing, and he asked Jamal what he needed a radio for if he had to play it so soft he couldn't hear it. Jamal figured a dead person could hear it the way Snookie played it.

Jamal was a little hungry. He had made some potatoes and chicken, but there wasn't too much of it. Sassy had eaten one piece of chicken, and he had had one piece. Sassy said she wanted two pieces because she wasn't going to eat any potatoes, but she knew better. They had to save something for Mama. If he had got the rice from Mr. Evans, he could have made the chicken and rice Mama liked a lot.

It was almost twelve o'clock when Mama got home. Jamal was in the bathroom when he heard the key in the door. He came out as quickly as he could. He saw that Mama had awakened Sassy and taken her into the bedroom.

"How come you didn't tell Sassy to go to bed?" Mama said.

"She wanted to watch television."

"She eat?"

"Uh-huh."

"What she eat?"

"That chicken from Sunday and some potatoes. We saved you some."

Mama went into the kitchen and looked at the food on the stove. She saw that Jamal had cut the potatoes into small squares and put some snap beans in with them.

"Where you get them snap beans?"

"They was in that plastic bowl in the back of the refrigerator," Jamal said.

"You get the mail?"

"Forgot," Jamal said. "You want me to go downstairs and get it?"

"No, I'm too tired to even read it," Mama said. She sat on the wooden chair, crossed one heavy leg over the other, and started to take her shoes off. Jamal liked the way Mama had looked before she had let her hair grow out. To him she had looked like the African women he had seen in magazines, strong and pretty and the same deep brown as he was. Her hair had grown out with patches of gray in the back and one just over her forehead. She looked older than before, before all the trouble with Randy.

"You stayed until five o'clock?"

"I stayed until visiting hours was up," Mama said. "Turn your head."

Jamal turned his head while Mama took her stockings off.

"How Randy doing?"

"I don't know," Mama said. "He still talking like he ain't got no sense, as far as I'm concerned."

"What he say?"

"He talking about how he gonna appeal his case and stuff, and asking me if I got five hundred dollars. No five hundred dollars grew on trees when he was out here in the street, and I sure don't see none growing on trees with him up there."

"He think he can get out?"

"I guess he ain't got nothing else to do up there except thinking about getting out," Mama said. She reached down and rubbed her ankle. "I sure hope this swelling in my feet go down by tomorrow," Mama said.

"You got some work?" Jamal said.

"Mr. Stanton call me just before I left to see Randy. He said he can give me two days this week. He said things may pick up for Christmas, too. Maybe I can get the money for Randy. I don't know."

"That other lawyer said he ain't getting out," Jamal said. "He said he can't get out until he do seven years."

Mama didn't say anything. She took a deep breath that seemed to swell her up, and then let it out slowly.

Jamal was sorry for what he had said, but it was true. Randy got fifteen to twenty years, and the lawyer said that he would have to stay in for at least seven years before he could come out on parole. When he got out, Jamal would be nineteen years old and Sassy would be fifteen. That was a long time.

He imagined Randy getting out, and meeting him. They might even be the same size, Jamal thought. He might even have a mustache by then.

CHAPTER TWO

When Jamal got up in the morning, the first thing he heard was the sound of Mama's gospel radio station coming from the kitchen. He looked at the clock on the end table. It was almost seven o'clock. He got up, wiped his eyes with his hands, and headed for the bathroom. Since Randy had gone to prison, he had moved out to the pullout bed in the living room and Sassy had the small bedroom all to herself.

He splashed water on his face, then decided to take a shower. He didn't remember about the hot water until after he had stepped into the bathtub. It had been off for two days. He turned the cold water on and stayed in the shower until it was too cold to stand, then hopped out. Sometimes, when the water wasn't really freezing cold, he could take a whole shower in the cold water.

Randy's stuff was still in the cabinet over the sink. Mama had brought his older brother all new stuff on her first visit to the upstate prison. Jamal put some of Randy's after-shave lotion on his hands, rubbed them together briskly, and then rubbed them on his face. He liked the way the lotion smelled.

He finished drying off, then went and got his clothes from where he had folded them neatly on a chair the night before. He dressed and went into the kitchen.

"Morning." Mama stood at the stove.

"Morning."

"Sassy up?" Mama asked.

"She wasn't up before," Jamal said. "I'll wake her up."

"She can sleep a little longer," Mama said.

"She can sleep all day if you let her," Jamal said.

"We ain't got no eggs." Mama had made tea and put a cup down for Jamal. The toast was already on the table. "You got on a clean undershirt?"

"Yes, ma'am."

Mama sat down across from Jamal and started putting sugar into her tea. She looked up when Sassy came out of her room.

"Morning, everybody," Sassy, her eyes still closed, said in a singsong voice.

"Morning, baby." Mama smiled when she saw Sassy in her Chinese pajamas. Sassy was eight, and coffee colored like her father, but she had wide eyes like Mama and Jamal.

"I said, 'Morning, *everybody*,'" Sassy said.

"My name ain't no everybody," Jamal said.

"Then how you know I'm talking to you?" Sassy said, her voice full of triumph as she made her way toward the bathroom.

"I hope you walk into the wall," Jamal said, seeing her eyes still closed.

Sassy went into the bathroom without walking into the walls and closed the door.

"I don't think she really got her eyes closed," Jamal said.

"You know what Randy said to me yesterday?" Mama said.

"What?"

"He said you should go and see Mack."

"I thought I couldn't go up there."

"Mack got out last week," Mama said.

"Oh."

"What you know about Mack?"

"I know he used to come here with Randy," Jamal said.

"Why you think Randy want you to see him?" Mama's voice rose ever so slightly, and Jamal looked up at her.

"I don't know," Jamal said. "What I'm supposed to see him about?"

"He just said he wanted him to tell you who to look out for in the Scorpions." Mama put another teaspoon of sugar in her tea. "Jamal, you ain't been hanging around the Scorpions, have you?"

"You know I don't hang around no Scorpions," Jamal said.

"I don't want you hanging around no Mack, either."

"I don't hang around nobody," Jamal said.

10

"You want some more toast?"

"Unh-uh."

Sassy came out of the bathroom and shuffled across the floor to her bedroom.

"Don't be taking all day to get dressed," Mama said.

"Can I wear my pink blouse?"

"Yeah, go ahead."

Sassy came over to the table and took a piece of toast. She took it with her to the bedroom. Jamal could never understand how his sister could eat toast with nothing on it.

A brown-and-white pigeon flew onto the ledge of the closed window. Jamal put his finger to his lips and then indicated the presence of the bird with a nod of his head. The pigeon walked from one side of their window ledge to the other. Jamal could see other pigeons lined up on the building across the street. They sat in groups of twos and threes, nearly motionless in the hard October sun, their gray bodies looking like stones on the edge of the roof.

"He don't even know we here," Jamal said softly.

"He know," Mama said.

There was something about Mama's voice, something that made her sound tired even though the day was just starting.

"You think I should give him some toast?" Jamal asked.

Before she could answer, another pigeon landed on the ledge, and then the two of them took off.

11

"Guess they don't want your toast," Mama said.

"You ain't going to drink that tea," Jamal said, smiling as his mother put more sugar into the cup.

"So what you going to do?" Mama asked, ignoring his remark about the tea.

"What you mean?"

"Mack. You going to see him?"

"What you want me to do?"

"Any of those Scorpions say anything to you?"

"No."

"Then why Randy want Mack to tell you who to look out for?"

"I don't know."

"Jamal Hicks, you lying?"

"No, ma'am."

Sassy came out of the bedroom in her blue skirt and pink blouse. She was greasing her hair.

"Why you got your good blouse on for?" Mama asked.

"You said I could wear it." Sassy stood at the end of the table holding her hair.

"Don't wear that blouse to school, Sassy."

"Why you say I could wear it if I can't?"

"I said you could wear it? Okay, go on."

Sassy gave her mother a look and went back into the bedroom to change her blouse.

"Jamal, you know I'm worried about that Mack boy," Mama said. "I don't think he right in the head."

"I ain't hanging out with him or nothing," Jamal

said. He counted the pieces of toast that were left. Three. He had had two already. He got up and got a drink of water.

"There's milk in the refrigerator," Mama said. "What you drinking water for?"

"Just wanted some," Jamal answered.

"So you ain't going to see Mack?"

"Unh-uh."

"Maybe you should, if Randy think somebody might bother you," Mama said.

"Maybe," Jamal said.

Jamal didn't like Mack. Mack was different from anyone Jamal had ever met. He had a strange way of talking, running his words together so that it was hard to understand him. Sometimes it seemed that he had trouble understanding things, too. Jamal had once seen Randy ask Mack what time it was and had seen Mack look at the clock and then say he didn't know. But more than anything it was the fights that Mack got into. The summer before Randy had got into trouble, Mack had been in juvenile home for breaking a man's arm with a baseball bat. The man had stepped on his shoes. Mama didn't know that, but Jamal did.

"He my ace," Randy used to say. "You get in a fight or something and you need an ace, man."

Mack had been with Randy and another guy named Willie Pugh when they pulled the stickup. According to the papers it was Randy and Willie who had gone into the delicatessen, with Mack outside as the lookout. Willie was only fourteen, so he went to juvenile court; Mack was fifteen, and Randy was the oldest at seventeen, and they were both tried as adults.

When the story got into the papers about the delicatessen owner being killed, everybody on the block was talking about it. Then Mack started bragging about how he had done it. Nobody believed Mack, not even the other Scorpions, but somebody dropped a dime on him and the cops picked him up. Jamal heard an old lady say that Mack was just foolish, maybe even addle headed.

"He gonna mess around," the dark, squat woman said, "and they gonna put that murder right on him."

Jamal thought she was probably right. He hadn't known then that Mack had been involved in the murder, and that Randy had been with him.

CHAPTER THREE

"Jamal, wait for Sassy so you can walk to school with her."

"I'm going to be late waiting for her," Jamal said.

"Sassy, put some Vaseline on your face before you leave," Mama said.

Sassy went into the bathroom. Jamal saw her standing in front of the sink and went to the bathroom door to watch her. She took some Vaseline from the jar, rubbed it between her palms, and then put it on her face. She made a tight face as she smoothed it on her cheeks, and squinted her eyes as she put it on the top of her nose. Then she turned toward Jamal and smiled.

"You think you cute or something?" Jamal asked.

"All I know is what I see in the mirror," Sassy said, walking past her brother.

"Mama, she think she cute," Jamal said.

"She is cute," Mama said.

"No she ain't."

"Tito think I'm cute," Sassy said.

"Tito told me you were ugly."

"No he didn't, 'cause he told Mary I was the cutest girl in the third grade."

"They must got some ugly girls in the third grade, then," Jamal said.

"Y'all get on to school." Mama patted Sassy's hair into place. "And don't fool around on the way."

•

The day started off wrong. Jamal had stopped to talk to Malcolm in the hall and was late for class. He had to go to the office and sit in there while the principal, Mr. Davidson, finished up some paperwork. Then he had to stand in Mr. Davidson's office and listen to him.

"How many times have you been late this year?"

Jamal shrugged.

"Look at me when I talk to you, young man."

Jamal looked up at Mr. Davidson and then back down at the floor. He knew he had been late four times. He had been late twice the week that Randy had been transferred from the city to the prison upstate.

"I would ask you to bring your mother to school, but she probably doesn't care any more about your education than you do."

Jamal felt tears coming to his eyes. He looked up at Mr. Davidson again, and this time he didn't put his head down.

"The very next time you're late, you're going to stay after school ten minutes for every one minute you're late. Do you understand that?"

Jamal didn't answer.

"I asked you if you understood it."

"Yeah."

" 'Yes,' " Mr. Davidson said. "At least try to talk as if you're civilized."

●

When Jamal walked out of Mr. Davidson's office, he felt like walking right out of the school. He was tired of school anyway. The only thing he did was to sit in the classrooms and listen to the teachers tell him what he couldn't do. He didn't even have to show up for school to know what they were going to say.

Mrs. Rich was checking the homework when he reached his first class. She was talking to Brandon about how he hadn't turned in his homework in three days.

Jamal wondered if she meant homework from the day before. He hadn't remembered any. He had even checked.

"Jamal, do you have your homework?"

"You didn't give out no homework yesterday," Jamal said.

Myrna Rivera giggled.

"You were supposed to have finished the workbook pages." Mrs. Rich stood up. "It was on the board for three days."

"It wasn't on the board yesterday," Jamal said.

"It was on the board in the morning," Christine said.

"Forget it, Jamal." Mrs. Rich went back to her desk. "I'm sure you like the seventh grade enough

17

to spend another year in it. Maybe you'll get some of your homework done by this time next year."

Jamal didn't say anything. Mrs. Rich was pretty good, but she was always on his case. She said he could do better if he really tried.

Reading was okay. He didn't get called on. Social studies was okay too. At least Mr. Hunter didn't bother anybody.

When Jamal got home for lunch, Sassy was already there. She liked to get home before him so she could unlock the door.

"Mama is working," she said.

"How you know?"

"The phone was ringing when I got in," Sassy said.

"She gonna be late?"

"No, she ain't working for Mr. Stanton. She doing some day's work. She said you should go down and get some eggs and bread, and we can have some egg sandwiches for lunch or some frankfurters," Sassy said. "I don't want no eggs."

"From Evans?"

"Yeah."

"I ain't going down there."

"Mama told me to tell you to go," Sassy said.

"I ain't going."

"I'm gonna tell Mama."

"I still ain't going."

"What we gonna eat for lunch?"

"I went down there yesterday to get some rice,

and he came loudmouthing me in front of everybody."

"What he say?"

"He ain't the welfare department."

"I ain't hungry anyway," Sassy said.

"This summer I'm getting me a job," Jamal said. "And I ain't spending nothing in his raggedy store."

"Me, too."

"You can't get no job," Jamal said. "It take a man to get a job."

"You ain't no man yet."

"You want to play some checkers?"

"Why, you feel like losing?"

•

Jamal got back to school on time, making sure to walk past Mr. Davidson so the principal would notice that he wasn't late. Mr. Davidson didn't say anything. That was what was wrong. When you did something wrong, everybody put their mouth on you. Then when you did something good, everybody acted like it wasn't anything special.

Grammar was his favorite class. He didn't actually like the subject, but Miss Brown wasn't too bad.

They talked about nouns and pronouns, and Mark Vibos got them mixed up again, as he always did. When the class was almost over, Miss Brown asked Jamal and Sandra if they could stay awhile after school and help get the stage ready for the seventh-grade play.

"We still have to paint the trees for the background," she said. "And I thought maybe we could even try to paint a park bench into the scene. I have two students from each of the other classes to help too. You can leave whenever you like."

"I'll stay," Jamal said.

Sandra said she could stay too.

"Good." Miss Brown smiled. She was the prettiest teacher in the school, even when she didn't smile. "There are a few other things to do as well."

If there was any one thing that Jamal could do, it was draw. He liked to draw and he liked to paint. Maybe for Christmas he would ask Mama to buy him some real paints, not the watercolors that you got at McCrory's. And a real paintbrush, too. He could paint with the brushes that came with the watercolor set he had, but what he wanted was a real artist's brush. Maybe even two, a big one that was flat on the end and a little one with a point.

The play was still three days off. If everything went okay between now and then, he would ask Mama to come and see the play. He'd have to find out who was coming, though, because he didn't want Mr. Davidson or anybody starting up anything with her. He would try to be real good until then. Do his homework every day and everything. Then he would ask Mama to come to the play, and she could see the trees and stuff he had painted.

He only had one more class, and that was guidance, with Mrs. Mitchell, his homeroom teacher. He looked at the clock on the wall. It was two minutes past two.

•

"Yo, Jamal, what kind of sneakers you wearin'?" They had just got into the guidance, and Dwayne was starting his mess again.

"Why don't you shut your mouth?" Jamal said. There were only fifteen minutes of school left, and he didn't want any garbage out of Dwayne.

"All I did was to ask you a question," Dwayne said, looking in the direction of Billy Ware. "What kind of sneakers you wearing?"

"None of your business," Jamal said.

"They look like Brand X sneakers to me," Dwayne said.

"I think you got a Brand X face," Jamal said.

"Hey, Billy, I think he got them sneakers from the Salvation Army."

Billy giggled and looked down at Jamal's sneakers.

"I got these sneakers from Bradley's," Jamal said.

"They look like they come from the garbage can behind Bradley's," Dwayne said. "You probably got that raggedy shirt from there too."

"If I put one of these sneakers upside your head, you won't worry about where they come from," Jamal said.

"You ain't got the heart, punk." Dwayne had a small head, and eyes that always looked half closed.

21

"You need your butt beat so bad you can't wait, huh?" Jamal said.

"You look like a frog," Dwayne said. "Anytime you feel like a frog, just leap on over here, 'cause I got something for you."

Dwayne looked around to see who was looking at him, saw Billy Ware watching them, and grinned.

Dwayne made Jamal feel small inside. Even when the older boy turned away from him, Jamal could still feel his grin. Lots of things made him feel the same way, small inside, and weak. The guy at the furniture store who had yelled at Mama had made him feel that way. Teachers who made him stand up in class when he made a mistake or didn't have his homework. Big kids who laughed at him were the worst because there wasn't anything he could do to stop them. Not by himself, not while he was small and not as tough as they were.

CHAPTER FOUR

Jamal ignored Dwayne for the rest of the period. It wasn't easy, especially when some of the girls started giggling. When the last period was finally over, he just got his coat and walked out. Later for Dwayne.

They had built a new stage in the auditorium over the summer, and it was nice. The back of it was higher than the front, and you could see everybody on it no matter where you sat. Miss Brown told everybody to sit in the front row while she got the materials. She asked Jamal to help her bring the paints in.

When they got everything in, Miss Brown went to the back of the stage and opened the curtains.

The trees were already drawn on the back wall and just needed painting. Miss Brown pointed to a large white area and said that it might be a good place to paint the park bench.

"I want Sandra and Evelyn Torres to work on painting the trees. I want Tara and Colin to do the park bench. Jamal, I want you to start opening all the windows so that they're open about a foot from the top. That'll air out the place. Then you can leave, Jamal."

He did it. He wasn't happy doing it, but he did it. Afterward he watched as the other kids drew the park benches and painted the trees in. He wasn't sure if he could have done it better, but he would like to have tried.

When he got home Sassy was making Kool-Aid.

"What you give me for some of my Kool-Aid?" she asked.

"Mama brought the Kool-Aid home?"

"I bought it," Sassy said.

"If Mama bought the Kool-Aid, I can get as much as I want," Jamal said.

"I told you I bought it," Sassy said.

"Where you get the money?"

"None of your B.I. business."

Jamal tried not to smile as he looked at Sassy's reader, which was on the table.

"Boy, this Kool-Aid sure is good," Sassy said. She had poured some in a cup and drank it and licked her lips.

"I think it looks like mud," Jamal said. "You like to drink mud?"

"It tastes so good I don't know what to do with myself," Sassy went on, ignoring him.

"Let me taste it so I can see how good it is."

"What you give me for some?"

"I don't want none anyway," Jamal said.

"You just said you wanted to taste it to see how good it was."

"You better save some for Mama."

"She bought six packs, so there's plenty left."

"I told you Mama bought it!" Jamal laughed.

"She bought six packs, but then she took them back and she gave me fifteen cents, so I bought this one pack all for myself."

"When I get some money I'll give you a quarter," Jamal said. "Give me some."

"A dollar."

"Okay, a dollar."

"Two dollars."

"You want to get rich on me or something?"

Sassy poured a large glass of Kool-Aid and put it on the table in front of Jamal, but her hand was still on it, ready to snatch it away.

"Two dollars," Jamal said.

"That's seventeen dollars you owe me," Sassy said.

"Mama okay?"

"Tired."

"Tell her I went to Tito's house."

"You better wait till she wakes up."

Sassy was probably right. He went to the refrigerator, opened it, and saw that Mama had bought a lot of food.

He went to the living room and started doing his homework.

Jamal could do the arithmetic when it just had regular numbers. But when it had fractions and decimals and stuff like that, it was hard. It wasn't that the arithmetic was just too hard for him, like it was for some of the kids; it was just that he couldn't remember all the rules.

Mrs. Rich had this big thing for minus numbers too. He didn't know why you had to have minus numbers. At first he thought it was like taking away, but it wasn't. He couldn't figure out why anybody would use a minus number when there couldn't even be such a thing.

Mama had got paid from the day's work and had shopped in the A&P. She made spaghetti and meatballs. That was just about Jamal's favorite supper.

After supper Jamal started washing dishes because it was his turn. That's the way they did things. One day Mama washed the dishes, one day Sassy did them, and then Jamal.

"I'll wash the dishes for you," Sassy said.

"Mama?"

"Okay if she want to," Mama said.

Sassy liked to wash the dishes because when she did Mama would dry them, and then they would talk like grown-up women.

"Can I go out?"

Mama looked up at the clock and then at Jamal. "You going to be back home when you supposed to be, or I'm going to have to go out and look for you like you some kind of criminal?"

"I'll be home," Jamal said.

●

Jamal took a notebook to the park and went up behind the playground. There was only one basketball game going on, and Jamal watched that for a while. Two old men sat in front of the park house playing cards. One of them was the old man who used to own the grocery store Mr. Evans owned now. When he had it he was okay, Jamal thought. He never gave anybody a hard time, and when people got their money they used to pay him. Everybody liked him. Nobody liked Mr. Evans. Most of the older people in the neighborhood went to the Spanish bodega on Manhattan Avenue.

Jamal started drawing trees to see how he would do on them. He did okay. He liked the way his trees looked. One of them came out really good, and he wished he had used plain white paper instead of the paper with blue lines. He turned to the back of his notebook, where he kept his wish list, and put down "plain white paper" right under "leather jacket."

•

The next day Miss Brown asked Jamal and Sandra if they wanted to stay awhile and help in the gym again. Jamal took out his notebook to show her his best tree.

"I can draw trees," he said.

"That's not bad," Miss Brown said. "The next time we draw trees, I'll ask you to help."

She smiled. Then she walked away.

•

Tito, his best friend, was waiting for him at the corner. He was sitting cross-legged on top of the

27

dark-blue post office box. A lot of the girls liked Tito. He had dark hair, and dark eyes that seemed almost too big for his face. But what the girls liked most was his long eyelashes. Tito didn't like girls and wanted to cut his eyelashes, but his grandmother had made him promise not to do it.

"So what you doing, man?"

"Just being cool," Jamal said.

"How come you didn't wear a coat?" Tito asked, jumping down from the mailbox.

"Just didn't. This sweater is warm enough, anyway."

"You want to wear my coat?" Tito had his books in a canvas bag and slung them from one shoulder to the other.

"Why I want to wear your coat?" Jamal asked as they crossed the street. Tito made a face at the girl crossing guard, who made a face back.

"I can wear your sweater," Tito said.

"You always wearing my stuff." Jamal smiled. "You a funny dude."

"That's what brothers do," Tito said. He was already taking off his jacket.

Jamal put his books down, slipped out of his sweater, and handed it over to Tito. It was too warm for a jacket anyway.

Tito had started borrowing Jamal's clothes right after they first met. It didn't have to be really nice stuff either. Jamal thought that in another year or two he was going to be bigger than Tito, but at the moment they were just about the same size.

"Hey, Tito, you got fifteen cents?" Celia Rodriguez was standing in front of the drugstore.

"Unh-uh."

"Jamal, you got fifteen cents?"

"If I give you fifteen cents, you gonna give me a kiss?" Jamal asked.

"You can get fifteen kisses for fifteen cents," Celia said.

"Too bad I ain't got it." Jamal shrugged.

"You just too cheap, Jamal Hicks." Celia waved her hand at Jamal. She went back into the drugstore.

"She like you, Jamal. I know she do," Tito said. "Every time she look at you, she smiles."

"She too tall. All them girls in the eighth grade too tall."

"You want to come to my house?"

"I got to check out Sassy first."

"Okay." Tito stopped and pointed across the street, where a fireman was standing directing a big hook and ladder truck out of the firehouse. The two boys watched as the truck moved carefully out onto the avenue, made a turn, and then, with a wail of its siren, started quickly uptown.

"I bet it's a false alarm," Tito said.

"You tell Sassy she cute?" Jamal asked.

"No, she say that?"

"I knew you didn't," Jamal said. "She always saying somebody said she cute or somebody said she smart."

Jamal rang the front doorbell twice before going through the open doors, as he always did. He checked the mailboxes and saw that they had received what looked like two bills, an advertisement from Macy's, and an official-looking letter from somebody. By the time he had checked the mail, Tito was already on the second floor, and Jamal had to run to catch up with him.

Jamal banged on the door with both fists.

"Who is it?" Sassy's voice came through the tin-covered door.

"Me."

The door opened, and Jamal and Tito went in.

"Mama home?"

"She call and said that she working for Mr. Stanton. She said that you supposed to clean up my room."

"You can say a lie faster than you can say the truth, girl."

"How you doing, Tito?" Sassy asked.

"Okay. Why you tell Jamal I said you was cute?"

"You don't think I'm cute?"

"You okay," Tito said.

"I didn't say nothing about no okay," Sassy said. "I said 'cute.' "

"Tell her she ugly," Jamal said. He put two pieces

of bread in the toaster and then opened the refrigerator to look for jelly.

"Okay, Tito." Sassy stood right in front of Tito. "You a Catholic, right?"

"What's that got to do with it?" Jamal put the jelly on the table.

"I ain't talking to you," Sassy said. She put her hand on her hip. "Now, Tito, are you a Catholic?"

"What's that got to do with it?" Tito asked.

"Be careful, man," Jamal said. "She's gonna get you."

"You shamed of being a Catholic?" Sassy asked, edging closer to Tito.

"No, I'm a Catholic," Tito said as he looked to see where Jamal was.

"And you ain't supposed to lie, right?"

"The truth is you ugly," Jamal said. He straddled the chair and sat down to see what Sassy was going to do.

"You ain't supposed to lie, right?"

"Yeah." Tito looked over at Jamal for help.

The toast came up, and Jamal went to get it.

"So what is the truth, Tito?" Sassy lowered her voice. "Am I cute or what?"

"You okay," Tito mumbled.

"Why you embarrassed?"

Jamal turned and looked at Tito. It was true, Tito was blushing. Jamal went over to him and messed his hair up and pushed his head down on the table.

31

"Just don't say she cute," Jamal said. "I'll give you both pieces of toast if you don't say she cute."

"It's all over his face," Sassy said. She put her head down on the table right next to Tito's. "Ain't it, Tito Cruz?"

"If you say she cute, you got to marry her," Jamal said. "You still got time to get away."

Jamal ran to the door and opened it. Tito looked up and saw him there, grabbed his books, and ran out of the door.

"Jamal, when you coming home?" Sassy called after her brother.

"Six o'clock," Jamal answered. "I'm going to do my homework over to Tito's house."

"You better be there if Mama calls," Sassy said.

"Shut up and lock the door, ugly."

•

"You should have told her she was ugly," Jamal said. "Only it don't make no difference, because she don't believe it anyway."

They walked down the avenue toward 125th Street, eating the toast. Jamal was mad at himself for not waiting to put the jelly on it.

"If Mama ain't working tomorrow, you want to come over to my house for supper?"

"Yeah. What you going to have?"

"How I know?"

"I don't care anyway, except if it's fish," Tito said. "I can't stand fish."

"When you got to be home?"

"Anytime," Tito said, smiling. "Abuela said I have to have more responsibility. So I can stay out later, but not too late."

"You get a letter from your dad?"

"Uh-uh. He's too busy. Abuela said it doesn't make any difference, because your grandmother is suppose to take care of you. She said in Puerto Rico everybody treats their grandparents like they were the real mother in the house. She said that your family is more important in Puerto Rico than here."

"You know, you got little teeth," Jamal said. "Open your mouth."

They stopped in front of a used-furniture store, and Tito opened his mouth so Jamal could look at his teeth.

"They nice, but the front teeth is kind of little," Jamal said.

"Let's see yours."

Jamal opened his mouth, and Tito looked at his teeth.

"Just your front two teeth are bigger than mine, I think," Tito said.

"Look, I got to go see Mack over on a Hundred and Twenty-sixth Street," Jamal said suddenly. "You want to come with me?"

"Now?"

"Yeah."

"Okay. Who's Mack?"

"This guy who was in my brother's gang." Jamal looked down the street toward where a couple was arguing in front of an empty lot.

"What you want to see him for?"

"Mama went to see Randy, and Randy told her to tell me to go see him."

"She went to the place to see Randy?"

"Yeah."

"You go?"

"No, you got to be fourteen or something like that," Jamal said. "Maybe even older. I don't want to see him in no prison anyway."

Three stray dogs—two small ones with scruffy black coats and a larger brown-and-white one with a tail that curled upward over his back—crossed the street. They came over toward a heavyset woman waiting for the downtown bus.

"Shoo!" The woman stamped her foot.

The large dog and one of the smaller dogs moved quickly away, but the other small one stood its ground and began to growl menacingly.

"Shake one of them big hips of yours at him!" a man sitting on the stoop called out. "That would scare me to death!"

The woman shot the man a mean look that shut him up and then looked back at the dog. The dog started to growl, looked around and saw that its companions were already headed past Jimmy's Cleaners, and went on his way.

"Randy gonna appeal his case?" Tito asked. "I told my cousin about him going to jail, and he said he could appeal his case."

"Why you got to go and tell him that?" Jamal stopped and looked at Tito.

" 'Cause . . . I don't know," Tito said.

"Man, you always talking too much."

"I'm sorry."

"You tell Abuela?"

"No."

"Yes you did."

"No, I didn't."

"If she say one word about him being in jail, I'm leaving your house and we never going to be friends again," Jamal said.

Jamal turned his head slightly so he could look at Tito from the corners of his eyes. He wanted Tito to know that he was serious.

"Come on," Tito said. "Don't be like that."

"You going to see Mack with me?"

"Yeah."

Jamal turned and started walking toward 126th. Tito started to follow at a distance without trying to catch up.

There was a group of older men standing in front of a barber shop. They talked loudly among themselves, stopping to look at a teenager carrying a boom box. One of the older men shook his head.

"That thing probably weigh more than he do."

The man was thin, with high, square shoulders. The sleeves of the topcoat he wore didn't quite come down to his wrists.

"You better mind your business, 'fore I go upside your head!" the teenager called out.

"Come on!" The thin man put his hand on his back pocket and left it there. The teenager looked at him sullenly, then walked slowly on. Tito caught up with Jamal.

●

The place Mack hung out in was mostly boarded over. Only one window was open, and that had a big cardboard ad for cigarettes on it. Over the door there was a sign—not a real sign, but the kind somebody who couldn't print straight had just painted on a piece of wood—that said "Video Games." From the street the place looked pretty dark.

Jamal had been there before with Randy. He knew it was a crack house. They messed with the stuff in the back, and then the teenagers took it around to sell.

Inside two guys were watching cartoons on television. One of them was wearing a beeper. Jamal nudged Tito and nodded toward it. The beeper probably meant the guy was a runner. That's how Randy used to make money sometimes. You could make a lot of money running crack. You just had to be sure you didn't start messing with it yourself.

There were two video game machines on one side of the small store, which had once sold groceries.

A few dusty cans of vegetables were spaced unevenly on the dusty shelves. Jamal looked at Tito. Tito's eyes were kind of wide, but he was there. That was the way Tito was. He got nervous sometimes, but he wouldn't let you down.

"What you boys want in here?" A heavyset man leaned across the counter and growled the words out.

"I'm looking for Mack," Jamal said.

"Mack who?"

"Mack from the Scorpions," Jamal said.

"He ain't around here" came the gruff reply.

"Where he at?"

"I ain't his father."

"I didn't say you was."

"You better get your fresh-ass mouth on out of here."

Jamal looked at the older man. Then he turned slowly and started out the door.

"You want to wait around here awhile?" Jamal asked Tito. "In case he come around?"

"I don't know," Tito said. "What time is it?"

"You can go on. I don't care."

"I'll wait with you."

They waited near the curb. Jamal leaned against a silver-gray Mercedes, and Tito sat on the curb next to him.

Jamal knew he didn't want to talk to Mack. Mack wasn't nothing but some trouble, like Mama said. He was the second oldest of the Scorpions too, but he didn't act like it. He acted like he was in the third grade or something. It wasn't what he did, so much; it was the way he talked. Jamal couldn't figure out why Randy even liked him.

Just before the jury had come back from making up their minds, and they called everybody into the courtroom, Randy had spoken to Jamal in the hallway. He said a lot of stuff about Jamal being the man of the house and how he had to take care of business if things went wrong for him.

"They ain't got no case, really," Randy was saying.

Jamal remembered Mama looking away from Randy. Mama was dark, like he was, and Jamal could see the tears running down her face. When they told them to come into the courtroom, the lawyer had to help Mama in.

Randy already knew things were going to go wrong for him because he knew he did the stickup and killed the guy. He had said Willie did it. He had said he and Willie was just walking in to buy something when Willie pulled out his gun and said it was a stickup. Mack had said the same thing. Willie had said he wasn't even there.

Jamal was mad at Randy, real mad. Mostly because of Mama crying and everything. When she got home at night from the trial, she would just sit and rock, and sometimes cry. She prayed a lot too, but that didn't help. Sometimes Jamal got mad at God, but Mama said he shouldn't be.

"God didn't shoot nobody," she said.

When the lady from the jury said that Randy was guilty, Mama started crying right out loud.

Jamal had looked at Randy. He was looking cool. Jamal hated that. You weren't supposed to be looking cool when you made your mother cry.

"How long you think he gonna be?" Tito asked as they sat in front of the boarded-up store.

"I said you can go if you want to," Jamal said, and walked over to the Mercedes.

Tito stood and leaned against the car, next to Jamal.

"I'm not going," Tito said. "I was just thinking, that's all."

A short, stocky man with a square head, dressed in a gray suit and a pink shirt, started into the store, then stopped and walked over to Jamal and Tito.

"Why you got to lean on my 'chine?"

Jamal looked at the car, then got off of it. Tito moved too. The man pushed Tito and almost made him fall.

"What you got to do that for?" Jamal said.

Jamal let his eyes move away from the man for a moment, then saw the big hand coming toward him, and felt it smack across his face.

"Catch you on my 'chine again, I'm gonna mess you up bad! You hear that?"

Jamal looked for something to hit the man with. One of the teenagers who had been in the store, the one without the beeper, came out and stood next to the man.

Tito had moved around the car, and Jamal, the taste of blood in his mouth, backed away.

"Why you let people mess with my 'chine?" the short man turned and snarled at the teenager.

The teenager, a tall skinny kid, backed away quickly from the shorter man. He looked over toward Tito and Jamal with anger in his eyes.

The teenager followed the man into the store, and Jamal looked for something to throw on the Mercedes.

"Hey, Jamal, what it is?"

Jamal looked up to see Mack, wearing the black-and-gold jacket of the Scorpions, headed toward them.

CHAPTER FIVE

Mack wanted to walk over to Marcus Garvey Park, but Tito said he didn't want to go to the park. Jamal didn't want to go into the park with Mack either. Instead they walked over to 116th Street. There were winos sitting on one bench, and Jamal, Tito, and Mack went to the other one.

"When you get out?" Jamal asked.

"Last week," said Mack. "This guy I know, he was going from Spofford to Green Haven, and I told him to look up Randy and tell him I was out."

"Randy said you turned him," Jamal said.

"No, man, I didn't turn him," Mack said, shaking his head. "Me and Randy always been tight. Willie the one done turned him. They got Willie on possession, and then he tried to cop him a plea by turning Randy and me. Only when they got me, I told them the truth, just like Randy told me. Willie done all the shooting. He was high. Randy told him not to get high, but he got high anyway."

"If you didn't turn Randy, why you out?"

"They let me cop 'cause I told them Randy and Willie was in there. Randy ain't mad about that, because they got the I.D. from the other lady who was in the store. I told them Willie did all the shoot-ing."

Tito was sitting on the back of the bench. He had his head back and his eyes narrowed.

"Yeah, that's what you say." Jamal looked down toward the playground, at two small girls in the swings.

"That the truth," Mack said.

"Randy said I should come see you."

"His lawyer call me and tell me that he can make a appeal for two thousand dollars," Mack said. "You know I ain't got that kind of dust, man. If I had it, I would shoot it on down to the lawyer so he could make the appeal."

"Two thousand?" Jamal remembered Mama say-ing that Randy needed five hundred dollars.

"Who he?" Mack nodded toward Tito.

"He my homeboy, Tito," Jamal said.

A red bus pulled up to the bus stop outside of the park, and a heavy lady got off. When she stepped down onto the sidewalk, Jamal saw that her legs were bowed. Her ankles were almost bent to the ground.

"Randy say maybe I can get the money from the Scorpions, but the Scorpions can't do no business if they mess with Randy," Mack said.

"How come?"

" 'Cause they don't want Randy out 'cause he too old. They don't want nobody seventeen or like that. If they have all young dudes like you and your homeboy here, then they can't get you to testify or nothing. Randy, he old. The man get him, then he got to turn somebody."

"I ain't got nothing to do with the Scorpions," Jamal said. "I don't run with no gang."

"You take over the Scorpions, then you can get the money for Randy's appeal," Mack said. "Randy told me that if he go down, you got to take his place."

"Take over the Scorpions?"

"Yeah, Randy say they can carry for the Spanish guys over near Ninety-sixth Street. They can make that money easy."

Jamal glanced over at Tito. Tito looked at him and then looked away.

"The Scorpions ain't just turning over their gang to me," Jamal said.

"Yeah, yeah they will. If I got your back, they got to give you some slack, 'cause I'm the Mack," Mack said. "I'm still the warlord. They don't mess with the Mack. You go in and you say you taking Randy's place. Then I got your back and everything be cool."

Jamal watched a small group of pigeons strut around a half-eaten corn muffin on the ground. A sparrow landed in the middle of them, poked at the muffin, and then hopped away as a pigeon pecked at him.

"You his boy—why don't you take over the Scorpions and get the money up?" Jamal asked.

"That ain't what Randy say," Mack said.

43

"I'm only twelve, man." Jamal sucked his teeth and looked away.

"You be twenty-one with what I got for you," Mack said. "I got the heat karate can't beat. Miss three five seven and a ticket right to heaven."

A blind man with a Seeing Eye dog crossed St. Nicholas Avenue. Jamal watched as the man followed the dog across the street. The dog looked happy taking the man around.

"I got to think about it," Jamal said.

"Randy said you got the heart."

"Yeah, he got the heart too. Look where he is."

"I got your back, so they ain't nothin to worry about. You and me is tight, just the way me and Randy was."

"Yeah. You be around here tomorrow?"

"I got to go see my parole officer tomorrow. I be around the next day."

"Okay." Jamal stood up. "I see you around then. How much you say he got to have?"

"Five hundred— two thousand," Mack said.

"What you mean? Five hundred or two thousand?"

"Yeah."

"Yeah?"

"You want me to bring that thing with me when I come?"

"No, not yet," Jamal said. "Me and Tito got to split. We see you outside that game room the day after tomorrow."

"I be there."

Jamal started walking uptown. Tito followed behind him. The wind was picking up, and it carried torn pieces of a Kentucky Fried Chicken bag against his legs and dust into his face. He walked onto Eighth Avenue without saying anything.

They went up 123rd Street to the drive, and then to the gray stone apartment building where Tito lived.

"How you feel?" Tito looked at Jamal.

"Okay."

"Don't look sad, okay?" Tito straightened Jamal's collar. "If Abuela see you looking sad, she gonna start asking questions and going on."

"Yeah."

"He mean a gun, right?" Tito said. "When he say he gonna bring something, he mean a gun, right?"

Jamal shrugged.

"Jamal, I don't like that guy. He act like he using crack or something."

"He always like that," Jamal said. "He don't never act right. That's why Mama didn't want him in the house."

"Why your brother like him?"

" 'Cause he stupid."

"Hey, try to look all right," Tito said as the elevator came.

A dark-haired Spanish girl with a big dog came out of the elevator, and the dog barked at Jamal. Jamal jumped back and the dog brushed by them.

"Your dog ain't nothing but a mutt," Tito said to the girl.

On the way up Tito asked Jamal what he was going to do, but Jamal just shrugged again. He didn't know.

●

Abuela said they had to eat. She warmed up some noodles and chicken, and they ate it with hot flat bread that Abuela made on top of the stove. It was good. Then they went to Tito's living room and started in on the homework. Tito had his comics under one of the pillows. They did part of the homework and started looking at Tito's comics.

"You can't take over no Scorpions," Tito said. "They got guys fourteen and fifteen years old. They're too old and too tough. They ain't gonna listen to a kid."

"I don't know. Mama was talking about getting some extra work to get the money for the appeal."

"Two thousand dollars?"

"She said only five hundred, something like that."

"If we could carry packages from the A&P, we could make maybe five dollars or seven dollars a day." Tito wrote down five and seven on the border of a comic. "That's twelve dollars if you made seven and I made five. That's every day twelve dollars. Then how many days we got to work to get to five hundred?"

"You mean carrying packages on Saturdays and Sundays, too?"

"Yeah."

"That's twelve dollars into five hundred dollars. It don't go even."

"How you know?"

"I don't think it go even because the last numbers are different."

Jamal figured out how many days it would take him and came up with forty-one days.

Abuela came in with cookies in little soup bowls. She asked Jamal if he played guitar, and he said that he didn't. Abuela was the same color as Tito, and her eyes were just as dark. But they didn't seem the same as Tito's. Abuela's eyes had creases in the eyelids, and they looked old. She always seemed happy, but she never smiled. To Jamal it was almost as if the old woman had a thousand things to do and never enough time to do them all. Jamal took the bowl of cookies and thanked Abuela.

"That's not too long," Tito said after Abuela had left.

"It's a little more, but that's about how long it take. We might as well do that," Jamal said. "They do everything so slow anyway. He was only seventeen when he got in that robbery, and then when the trial come up he was eighteen already."

"I think that's better than messing with the Scorpions," Tito said.

"I got to make sure how much money they need for the appeal."

"How you going to do that?"

"Call up the lawyer. I had to do that once when they first started out because we had to know how to get to the courtroom."

"We could make more on weekends, and it wouldn't even be that long," Tito said. "Suppose we got lucky and carried this real heavy package for a rich lady. Then she say, 'Oh, here's a hundred dollars for each of you.' "

"No, suppose she say her husband a lawyer and he'll do the appeal for us if we carry her groceries all the time."

"That could happen," Tito said.

"Yeah, but you know where that got to happen? In one of them big white stores downtown."

Abuela came in again, this time with milk, and called Tito "Tito Gordito."

"Tell Jamal what that means in English," Abuela said as she left the living room.

"What it mean?"

"Little fat Tito."

"You want to finish the homework now?"

"No."

"See, that's why I can't get my homework done," Jamal said. "We supposed to be doing it and you don't want to."

"You want to finish it now?"

"You didn't want to finish it first," Jamal answered.

"Okay, I'm going to tell the teacher—if she calls on me, because most of the time she don't call on me—that a crazy mugger took my homework."

"Why a mugger going to take your homework?" Jamal said. "That don't make no sense."

"See, I said he was crazy." They both laughed.

"I got to go," Jamal said. "But your grandmother is right. You getting as fat as a girl."

"I'm not that fat."

"You getting kind of fat."

"Jamal, I don't think you should mess around with no gun, man," Tito said. "When I think about that, it makes me sad."

"How I'm gonna tell the Scorpions what to do?"

"I don't know," Tito said. "Randy, he shot somebody and kill them. Maybe they think you going to shoot somebody and kill them too."

●

"Guess who I run into yesterday?"

"Who?"

"Mack."

"Where you run into him?" Mama put down the dish towel and turned toward Jamal.

"Over near St. Nicholas."

"What you doing over there?"

"Just walking."

"Just walking my foot! When you think I was born? Sometime this morning?"

"No, ma'am."

"I don't want you near that boy, you understand me, Jamal Hicks?"

"Yes, ma'am."

"And I don't want his name mentioned in this house. If Randy wasn't out fooling around with that lamebrain— You know he ain't right, don't you?"

"He don't act right."

"So what you soupin' up to him for?"

"I told you I just run into him."

"Don't you 'told' me nothing, fresh mouth."

Sassy came out of her bedroom and sat down at the table.

"What you want, Sassy?"

"You said that we shouldn't have no family secrets, Mama."

"Sassy, you can stay out here, but keep your mouth shut."

"I wasn't going to say nothing," Sassy said. "He can hang out with any kind of hoodlums he wants for all I care."

"Sassy, go to your room!"

"Mama, all I said was—"

"Girl, if I take my shoe off, you going to wish you had your hind parts in your room!"

Sassy shot Jamal a look and went to her room.

Mama turned back to her cooking. She had spent nearly an hour washing the mustard greens, cutting up the streak of lean to put in them, and boiling pork tips in vinegar and water.

Jamal didn't say anything anymore about Mack. What he wanted was to ask Mama for the lawyer's card so he could call him and find out how much it would cost for the appeal. It had cost nearly seven hundred dollars for the lawyer to begin with. Randy hadn't wanted the public defender.

There was a radio on somewhere in the building playing gospel songs.

"They got some gospel music on the radio," Jamal said. "You want me to find it for you?"

Mama looked over at Jamal, then looked away back to her greens. Then she went over to the radio, put it on, and started searching for the gospel music. After a while she found it, took a step away from the imitation leather radio, then turned back to it and cut if off.

"What Mack say?" she asked.

"Nothing much."

"Boy, you got to know this thing is cutting into my heart like a knife. Now don't you play with me, because I just cannot stand it. As God is my secret judge I don't *need* to be played with."

"He said that the lawyer called him and said he needed money for the appeal. But he said it was two thousand dollars."

"What kind of lawyer be calling him?"

"That's what he said."

"Two thousand dollars?"

"I thought about calling the lawyer and asking him."

Mama started humming to herself. Jamal knew she was doing some heavy thinking when she started humming to herself.

"I don't know why Randy told you it was five

hundred and the lawyer told Mack it was two thousand," Jamal said.

"One day it's five hundred dollars, then the next day it's a thousand dollars, and the next day it's two thousand dollars," Mama said with a sigh. "They know you love these children and you got to do what you can. What else Mack say?"

"Nothing."

"Jamal?"

"What I want to talk to him for?" Jamal said.

"You just keep it in your head that that boy ain't had no upbringing and don't amount to two cents. And that's what God loves, the truth."

"You want to call the lawyer?"

"I'm thinking about trying to borrow the money from Mr. Stanton," Mama said.

Jamal turned away. The last time Mama borrowed money from Mr. Stanton, to pay for Randy's lawyer and to buy him a new suit so he would look good at the trial, she had had to work for him almost six months for nothing to pay the loan off.

"I could get an afternoon job," Jamal said.

"You want to call the lawyer, go ahead," Mama said.

"Where his card?"

Mama went and got the lawyer's card from her dresser. Jamal looked at it, then started dialing the number. When he had finished, Mama took the phone from him. She tapped her foot and hummed while she waited for someone to answer.

"I'd like to speak to Mr. Addison, please," she said. "It's about the Randy Hicks case.

"Hello? Mr. Addison? This is Mrs. Hicks. I'm calling about my son Randy."

Mama nodded as she listened to the voice on the other end of the phone. Behind her Sassy was putting the pot on for tea.

"No, he already been on trial," Mama said. "He got from fifteen to life. He's tall and brown skinned . . ."

Mama was listening again.

"They say he shot a man." Mama's voice dropped. She listened again.

"That's right. That's right. That's him. He said you told him he could get an appeal for five hundred dollars, and . . ."

Mama motioned for Sassy to bring her something to write on. Sassy brought her a ballpoint pen and a piece of theme paper.

"I see . . . I see. . . . And bring the money down to you?"

Mama nodded again, and then hung up the phone.

"What he say?" Jamal searched Mama's face.

"He say he don't know if it can go through, but he can make an appeal. It's going to cost about two thousand dollars, but he'll start it with five hundred dollars."

"I thought Randy could get a free lawyer," Sassy said.

"Mr. Addison said he could try that if he want,

53

but he didn't sound like he had much faith in it," Mama said. "And how you going to say no if he say he think he might get Randy out?"

"Two thousand dollars is a lot of money," Sassy said.

"The lawyers got to get their money too," Mama said.

"What you gonna do?" Jamal asked.

"Got to try to get it together, what it takes," Mama said. Her eyes were shiny, and Jamal thought she might cry. "Jamal, you mind making some hamburgers for you and Sassy?"

"It's too hard on you, Mama," Sassy said. Jamal had never seen Sassy cry so fast over anything. "It's too hard."

"One day"—Mama's eyes looked far away—"I was walking downtown with Randy in my arms. I was waiting for a light to change when this white lady stopped and looked at him. I looked at her and she was smiling and I smiled back at her, and that was the best feeling in the whole world. You got a baby and you hope so much for it. . . ."

"I'll make the hamburgers," Jamal said.

Mama went into the bedroom, and Jamal could hear the bedsprings under her weight. That was what the whole thing with Randy was doing to her— making her tired, making her just want to lie down and go to sleep.

"I hope Randy get out soon," Sassy said.

"I hope he don't never get out," Jamal said.

"I'm going to tell Mama you said that."

"Don't you tell her that," Jamal said.

"I will."

"If you do I'm going to punch you in your face."

"I'm going to tell her you said that, too," Sassy said. "Mama!"

"Go on," Jamal said. "Make her feel worse. You don't care."

"What you want, Sassy?" Mama's voice came from the other room.

"She don't want nothing," Jamal said. He waved his finger in front of Sassy's face.

"Don't you tell me what I want!" Sassy's voice rose. Jamal heard the bedsprings again as Mama got up.

"Can't you children get along for two minutes?" Mama stood in the doorway. When she had her shoes off she wasn't much taller than Jamal.

"Jamal said he hope Randy don't never get out of jail."

"Jamal! How you fix your mouth to say something like that, boy?" Mama's voice cracked, and her face tensed so that Jamal could see her teeth. "How you fix your mouth to say that, boy?"

The tears were coming down Mama's face, and Jamal turned away from her. "I'm sorry," he said.

"Lord Jesus!" Mama said. "Lord Jesus, what is this family coming to?"

Jamal looked up as Mama went back into the bedroom.

"You ain't so big now, are you," Sassy said.

Jamal looked up at her. "At least I didn't say nothing to Mama to make her cry," he said.

He went into the bathroom and closed the door. He took his pants down and sat on the toilet. The top of his legs spread out against the white toilet seat.

It was true. He didn't want to see Randy again. Randy was always making Mama cry. Everything his brother did just seemed to be wrong. And Randy didn't even know how Mama felt. Or maybe he didn't even care—Jamal didn't know. He had got into trouble with the police before, and Mama had had to go to the court and miss work because of him.

Then what did Randy say when he come home? Some jive stuff about how he was too slick for the police. Mama was crying all night long when they had Randy out in New Jersey in the youth house, and she had to borrow money and everything just to get him out.

Jamal took some toilet tissue and wiped the tears away from his face.

This mess was the worst, he thought. If Randy got out again, he was just going to do some more messing up. Jamal just knew he would.

"Jamal?" Sassy's voice.

"Get out of here."

"I got to pee."

Jamal thought about just ignoring Sassy, but then he figured she would just go in and bother Mama again, so he got up, pulled his pants up, and opened the door.

Sassy was standing in the doorway.

"I'm sorry."

"Oh, shut up!"

"You the one that—"

Jamal shut Sassy up with a look. She went into the bathroom and closed the door.

Jamal washed his hands and went to the refrigerator. There were three hamburger patties in a neat pile next to the milk. He glanced over at Mama's door. He figured she wouldn't eat anything. He took out one hamburger for Sassy. He wasn't hungry either.

CHAPTER SIX

"I bet I can get down to the second floor before you do." Oswaldo Vazquez had been standing at the top of the stairs, and Jamal was already halfway down. He knew what Ozzie was going to do. He would jump down the first flight, then jump down the second while Jamal was running.

"Bet!" Jamal said.

Ozzie and Jamal jumped at the same time. Jamal lost his balance a little but got to the second flight at the same time that Ozzie did. They both jumped at the same time again and landed together at Mr. Davidson's feet. . . .

There was a picture of George Washington over Mrs. O'Connell's desk, and a picture of Martin Luther King over Mrs. Rose's desk in the office. Jamal and Ozzie had been sitting in the principal's office all morning with their hands folded in their laps.

Jamal looked at the pictures and wondered why the one of George Washington wasn't finished.

At eleven o'clock Mr. Davidson called Jamal and Ozzie into his office.

"Oswaldo, you have a fairly decent record." Mr.

Davidson held a folder in his hand. "Why are you associating with somebody like Hicks?"

Ozzie shrugged and looked down at his shoes.

"I'm giving you two warnings, Oswaldo," Mr. Davidson said. "The first one is that if I get any more complaints about you this term, especially about you fooling around in the hallway, you're going to find yourself in a lot of trouble. Do you understand that?"

"Yes, sir." Oswaldo spoke quietly.

"The second warning is that if you continue to find people like Jamal Hicks for your friends, you're going to be in trouble if you like it or not. Do you understand that?"

"Yes, sir."

"You can go."

Oswaldo stood quickly and left without looking at Jamal.

"I'm not going to give you a warning because I don't think it's going to do you any good," Mr. Davidson said to Jamal. "So you just go on and do what you want to do. Sooner or later you're going to do something that's going to let me put you out of the school. You know that and I know that. Go on to your classroom."

They were collecting homework when he went into the room, and Jamal turned his in. Then they started talking about how the government was divided up into three parts. The teacher called on

59

Jamal and asked him if he could name the third part, after Tamia Davis has said the Supreme Court and the Congress.

"The executive," Jamal said.

Dwayne cracked up. "It's the president, stupid," he said.

"Jamal is right, it's the executive branch, of which the president is the head."

Jamal looked over at Dwayne. Dwayne was still laughing. Even though the teacher said that Jamal was right, Dwayne was acting as if he were wrong.

The class went on, and Dwayne kept looking back at Jamal and laughing. He got Billy to laugh too. The only way to deal with somebody stupid like Dwayne, Jamal thought, was to punch him out. Dwayne always acted so tough, and he thought Jamal was scared of him, but he wasn't. He wasn't scared of anybody.

●

Jamal waited on the corner until Tito showed up. Tito had on one of Jamal's shirts.

"Why you wearing my shirt to school?" Jamal asked.

"This ain't your shirt," Tito said. "This used to be your shirt, but now it's mine because I wear it more than you do."

"That's because you don't give it back," Jamal said as they walked down the street.

"You got to go right home?" Tito asked.

"Unh-uh."

"Let's go over to the boat place."

"All the way down to Seventy-ninth Street?"

"Yeah."

"Okay."

It took Jamal and Tito almost an hour to get down to the boat basin, but it was worth it. It was mid-October, and soon there wouldn't be many boats around, but there were still a few now.

Tito started coughing. Jamal hated it when Tito coughed. It seemed as if there was something in Tito's chest that made him swell and that he was trying to get out. When he coughed really hard, Tito's eyes would roll around and glisten with his efforts. Jamal put his arm around Tito's shoulders.

This time the coughing didn't last that long, and soon they were going along the walk picking out boats, the way they always did.

"See that one?" Tito pointed out a small boat with black-and-gold trim.

"Yeah?"

"That's going to be my first boat," Tito said. "I'm going to get one just like that, and then later, when I get really rich, I'm going to get that big one over there."

"What you going to do with the little one?" Jamal leaned over the side of the rail.

"Maybe I'll give it to my wife or something," Tito said.

"Suppose you ain't married?"

"Then maybe I'll give it to a poor kid."

"I'm going to get a big boat first," Jamal said.

"You ought to save your money first."

"Suppose there's a war or something and they start dropping bombs and everything? What you think they gonna bomb first?"

"They ain't going to bomb the boats, man. No way."

"Yes they are. They gonna bomb everything the rich people got."

"Maybe."

A man in a blue jacket and white sailing cap came from below deck on one of the boats. Tito nudged Jamal. Then they both waved to the man.

The man waved back. The boys watched as he went about the boat checking things, then climbed over the side onto the pier.

"Let's go ask him how much the boat cost," Tito said.

"He won't even tell us."

"You scared?"

Jamal gave Tito a look and pushed away from the railing they were leaning against. Tito didn't catch up with him. Jamal knew that Tito was the one who didn't like talking to strangers. It didn't bother him.

"How much your boat cost?" he asked when they had reached the man.

"Thinking of buying it, are you?" The man was taller than he had looked on the boat. He had a sharp nose, gray-blue eyes, and just the beginning of a small beard.

Jamal smiled and looked at the boat. "I just want to know how much it cost you."

"It's not really my yacht," the man said. "The company I work for owns it, but I get to use it."

"Anybody in your company can just ride on it when they want to?"

"Not anybody," the man said. "But I can."

"How much it cost?" Tito spoke up.

"I would think in the neighborhood of about eighty-five thousand dollars."

"I might get me one when I get a job," Jamal said.

"Good luck with it." The man touched the front of his cap and started off.

"That's a lot of money," Tito said. "He's probably rich. He looks rich."

"He ain't that rich," Jamal said. " 'Cause he working for a company. If he was real rich, he would have his own boat."

"His own yacht," Tito said.

"Yeah. You know that got a *c* in it?"

"What?"

" 'Yacht' got a *c* in it," Jamal said. "I saw it in a reader."

"I think we ought to go on home now," Tito said.

"You got asthma?"

"A little."

"You got carfare to go home?"

"Unh-uh. You?"

"Unh-uh."

They walked downtown to 72nd Street and Broadway. They were thinking of sneaking on the train there, but there were two cops standing near the booth. One was white, the other black.

"My friend got asthma," Jamal said. "Can we get on the train 'cause he can't walk all the way uptown?"

"Get out of here!"

"You don't gotta be nasty about it," Jamal said to the black cop.

"What are you, a wise guy?"

The white cop tapped Jamal lightly with his nightstick. Jamal pushed the nightstick away and glared at the cop.

Tito started coughing again. He took Jamal's arm and began to pull him away from the two cops.

Jamal pulled his arm from Tito's grasp.

"You see he got the asthma," Jamal said.

"Get out of here!" The white cop waved his hand toward the gates, and Jamal took Tito's arm and pulled him through.

Tito coughed a lot on the way uptown. A woman gave him a packet of tissues.

"You know what we could do if we were rich?" Jamal said. "We could go live someplace warm, and maybe you wouldn't get asthma all the time."

"We could live in Puerto Rico," Tito said.

"We could get us a boat and drive to Puerto Rico."

"If we had two boats, we could race."

"Why?" Jamal answered. "You getting that little boat and I'm getting the big boat, so you know I would win."

"Yeah, I forgot," Tito said.

CHAPTER SEVEN

Mama had burned her hand real bad in the morning. Sassy had been getting ready to go to school when she opened her schoolbag and all of her crayons fell out. They started rolling around the floor, and some rolled under the ironing board. Mama was ironing Jamal's shirt.

"What you doing, girl?" Mama shouted as Sassy started scrambling around on the floor picking up the crayons.

Jamal saw the whole thing happen, just like a movie. Sometimes he saw things like that.

First Mama started to look over the ironing board to see where Sassy was. Then she hit the cord to the iron with her arm and the iron fell over. It wasn't going to fall off the ironing board, but Mama grabbed it anyway. She grabbed it with her bare hand and pulled it away from the edge of the board.

"Sassy, move!"

"I'm just getting my crayons!" Sassy said.

But Jamal had already seen Mama jerk her hand away from the iron.

"You okay, Mama?"

Mama stood the iron up with her other hand and held on to the handle.

"What's wrong?" Sassy stood up.

Mama was shaking her hand. Then, when she saw that Sassy wasn't going to be burned, she went over to the sink and ran some cold water over the burn. Jamal didn't look at Mama's hand. He looked at her face.

Mama's teeth were tight together and her eyes were closed.

"Mama?" Sassy turned her head to one side so she could see Mama's face too.

"It ain't nothing, girl," Mama said. "Get on to school before you be late."

Jamal didn't say anything. He put his shirt on real fast so Mama wouldn't try to finish ironing it. It looked okay anyway.

●

Dwayne started some mess in school. First Myrna got in trouble for blowing a bubble in the classroom. Myrna was always doing things and not getting caught, but this time Mrs. Rich caught her blowing the bubble.

Then Myrna started saying stupid things about Mrs. Rich, about how short her hair was and stuff. Then Dwayne started. Nobody paid him any attention. Then he started on Jamal.

"How come your shirt look okay in the front and all wrinkled up in the back?" he said, making sure everybody could hear him.

"How come your face is all wrinkled up?" Jamal said.

Dwayne kicked him from across the aisle. Jamal waited until Mrs. Rich was facing the board, and then he kicked Dwayne back as hard as he could on the back of his leg.

"I'm gonna punch you in your eye, faggot!" Dwayne stood up.

"Sit down!" Mrs. Rich's voice cut through the classroom.

"He kicked me!" Dwayne said.

"I didn't kick him."

"I'm gonna get you outside." Dwayne sat down. He was nodding his head, and then he started punching his fist into the palm of his hand.

Jamal wasn't scared of Dwayne. He had already fought Dwayne once. Everybody said that Dwayne won the fight because Jamal had a cut lip. But Jamal had got Dwayne two times in the face, and it was Dwayne, even though he was a lot bigger than Jamal, who had stopped fighting first.

In science they saw a movie. It was about water pollution. One part showed birds covered with oil on a beach. The oil was so thick that the birds couldn't fly.

"That's Jamal's mama." Dwayne's voice came from the back of the room.

●

Jamal didn't feel like fighting.

"Let's just go," Tito said.

"I ain't gonna punk out."

"He too big."

"I don't care."

Dwayne came down the street with Billy Ware, Myrna, and Ralph Williams. Jamal gave Tito his books to hold and then crossed his arms in front of him.

"Fight!" Myrna called out, and some kids from across the street started crossing over.

"So why you kick me, fool!" Dwayne stood as close as he could to Jamal.

" 'Cause I did!" Jamal said.

Dwayne pushed Jamal and Jamal pushed him back. Then Dwayne kicked Jamal just below the knee.

The pain was sudden, and Jamal bent over to grab his knee. Dwayne hit him on the back of his head, and Jamal grabbed Dwayne around the waist.

Dwayne was almost fourteen, big, and he could hit hard. He kept punching Jamal in the back, but Jamal wouldn't let go of his waist. He tried to hold Dwayne and kick his legs, but he couldn't reach them. Then he started forward, forcing Dwayne back faster and faster until they stopped. Jamal could see that they had fallen against a car.

Dwayne tried to turn Jamal around and get him up against the car. Jamal grabbed Dwayne's leg and lifted it and pushed forward again. Dwayne slid along the car and then went down.

On the ground Jamal let go of Dwayne and started

punching. Dwayne got him in the face twice, and he swung back at Dwayne's face. They were lying on the ground punching and Dwayne was trying to kick him when two men pulled them apart.

"You guys got nothing better to do than tear your damn clothes up?"

Both the men were mailmen. Jamal looked at his shirt and saw that it was torn.

"Hey, Dwayne," Myrna called out. "You got doo-doo on your pants."

Dwayne looked at his pants and turned back toward Jamal when he saw what was on them.

"I'm gonna get you again tomorrow!" Dwayne was saying.

"You go that way!" One mailman pointed down the street and pushed Dwayne in that direction. "And you go that way!"

•

"You okay?" Tito was waiting for Jamal.

"Yeah," Jamal answered. "Look, loan me your sweater so my mother don't see how I tore my shirt."

Tito took off his sweater and gave it to Jamal.

"I think you won the fight," Tito said. "He don't hit so hard, right?"

"He hit pretty hard, but I got some in too."

"And he the one that rolled in that dog doo."

"I wish his face had rolled in it."

"What you going to do if he start up tomorrow?"

"Start up with him."

70

Mama wasn't home. Sassy was in her room, and Jamal went straight to the bathroom. He took the shirt off and looked at it. Dwayne had torn his pocket off and ripped the shirt right down the front. Jamal's face hurt too, and he had a bruise on his elbow that he hadn't noticed before.

"Jamal, you in there?"

"Yeah."

"Come out!"

"Why?"

"I got to pee."

"Shut up!"

"Come on out! I got to pee!"

Jamal opened the door and came out.

"What happened to you?" Sassy asked.

"Nothing."

"Don't tell me nothing."

"I thought you had to pee."

"I don't have to pee now."

"Where Mama?"

"She went to work for Mr. Stanton," Sassy said.

"How her hand?"

"Messed up. She put some lard on it, and then she put a bandage on it."

Sassy started doing her homework on the kitchen table. Jamal went into Sassy's room and opened the closet. Jamal went through it until he found Randy's old Scorpions jackets. Randy had two

Scorpions jackets; one was larger than the other. It was the smaller one that Jamal tried on. It was still a little too big for him, but not by much.

●

Everybody was talking about the fight when Jamal got to school the next day. Dwayne had reached school first and was talking about how he had beat up Jamal.

"He looks okay to me," Myrna said when she saw Jamal.

Oswaldo Vazquez said that the fight had been even, and most of the kids who liked Jamal said it was. The ones who liked Dwayne said that he had won.

Jamal didn't think the fight was even. He thought he had probably lost it, but it didn't mean anything to him. He knew he couldn't fight his best when he was thinking about Mama and getting Randy out of jail and stuff like that. Some of the girls started in giggling and pointing to him, but he just let it go.

"We gonna have to settle this mess," Dwayne said when they reached math. "You gonna punk out?"

"I'll be there," Jamal said. "Just bring your butt so I can kick it again."

Dwayne had called him out in front of everybody like he was in a movie or something, Jamal thought. That's how Dwayne was getting off, like a cowboy. Jamal told himself that this time the fight would be different. He was going to try to tear Dwayne's shirt, and then, instead of grabbing him around the waist, he was going to go for his face right away.

"Today we're going to study decimals," Mrs. Rich was saying. "Who can tell me where the word 'decimal' comes from?"

The night before, Mama hadn't got home until almost ten thirty. Jamal and Sassy had been worried. Sassy didn't even fall asleep, the way she usually did. When Mama got home, she had some Kentucky Fried Chicken and french fries.

"How come you so late?" Sassy asked.

"Mr. Stanton let me work until nine fifteen. As slow as I was working with this hand, I wouldn't have made no money quitting at five thirty."

"Your hand bother you a lot?" Jamal asked.

"It's okay," Mama said. "I take this bandage off and let it get some air, it'll be okay in the morning."

Jamal looked over at Sassy. It had been her fault, her and her stupid crayons all over the floor, that Mama had burned her hand in the first place. Sassy had given him a look right back.

"Jamal, do you *ever* think there will be a day when you pay attention in this class?" Mrs. Rich asked.

"Yes, ma'am."

"So can you give me the decimal for the fraction five tenths?"

"No, ma'am."

The day took forever. He saw Tito in the hallway, and Tito said that he had changed his mind about the boats. Now he was going to buy the big boat first too.

"Too late, now," Jamal said. "You already said you were gonna buy the small boat."

"I'm going to buy the same size boat that man was on," Tito said.

"I'm getting a boat bigger than that," Jamal said. "So I'm still going to beat you to Puerto Rico."

"Not if my father's on my boat," Tito said. "Because he knows all about how to get to Puerto Rico."

"So I can get me a map."

"He don't need a map."

"You going to wait for me outside?"

"Yeah."

•

Jamal forgot about the fight with Dwayne until the last period, when Dwayne started up again. Dwayne pushed Jamal as they walked into the classroom.

"Dwayne, what is your problem?" the teacher asked.

"I don't have a problem." Dwayne had this big smile on his face and was looking around.

"Well, I think you do." Mrs. Mitchell was tall, with gray-blue eyes. "And you can just stay after school until you solve it."

"I can't stay this afternoon," Dwayne said. "I got something to do."

He looked at Jamal, and a few of the other kids started laughing.

"You'll stay," Mrs. Mitchell said.

During the class Dwayne whispered something to Billy, and Jamal saw Billy writing a note. Billy put it on Jamal's desk, but Jamal just pushed it off.

When Mrs. Mitchell left the class to get some ditto sheets, Billy turned to Jamal.

"Dwayne want to know if you going to wait for him outside," Billy said aloud.

"Or you gonna run like a punk?" Dwayne asked.

"I'm going to run over to your house and see your mama," Jamal said.

Dwayne threw his spelling workbook at Jamal. The pages opened, and it fluttered through the air as Mrs. Mitchell came in.

"Dwayne, did you just throw that book?"

"I went to hand it to—"

"Quiet!" Mrs. Mitchell shut Dwayne up.

●

Jamal stood on the corner after school. He knew that Dwayne had to stay until at least three thirty. He wasn't sure if he was going to wait for him or not. He wanted some of the kids to see him there so they wouldn't say he was too scared to show up.

"Yo, Jamal!"

Jamal looked up to see Mack.

"What's happening?"

"Let's take a walk. I got something for you," Mack said.

"I got to wait for Tito."

"I got to go down the block," Mack said. "I can't be near the school or nothing. I'll be on the next corner."

"How you know I went to this school?" Jamal asked.

"Me and Randy did some business around here once," Mack said. "He told me."

Mack walked on, and Jamal leaned against a pole. At the top of the pole there was a yellow sign that said, "Watch Out for Children."

"You waiting for Dwayne?" Billy had his books in a new bookbag.

"Get out my face."

"I just asked you a question," Billy said.

Jamal pushed away from the pole, and Billy started walking.

Jamal thought about Mack waiting for him down the block. He had a bad feeling about Mack, a real bad feeling. Jamal glanced up toward his homeroom. He felt Dwayne would be there, looking down at him, but he wasn't.

Tito came.

"Hey, I heard you were going to fight Dwayne again."

"He started some more mess."

"You waiting for him now?"

Jamal shrugged.

"You want me to help you fight him?"

"Unh-uh. I got to go anyway. Mack is down the street waiting for me."

"Who?" Tito asked as they started down the street. Most of the kids from school had already left. No one was supposed to stay in front of the school after three, but a few were still standing around.

"You know, that guy we met crosstown."

"Oh."

Jamal looked at Tito. "Why you say 'oh' like that?"

"Like what?"

"Like . . . just like 'oh,' " Jamal said.

"That's the way I always say 'oh.' "

Mack was standing on the corner and motioned for Jamal and Tito to follow him. They followed him down the street at a distance until he stopped and went into a building.

"What he want?" Tito asked.

"I don't know. Probably something about the Scorpions."

"You can't be a Scorpion," Tito said, shaking his head.

"How come?"

" 'Cause you going to get in trouble," Tito said. "That's what I think."

"If I start to be a Scorpion, you want to be in the gang?"

"What you got to do to get in?"

"I'll just let you in."

77

"Okay."

"I thought you said I couldn't be no Scorpion," Jamal said, smiling.

"I don't think you should be," Tito said. "But if I'm in the Scorpions, maybe we can get them to do some good things too."

"And we can look out for each other," Jamal said.

●

The building that Mack went into was old. The mailbox in the small hallway was dented, and the plaster chipped away from one corner.

"There's a meeting of the Scorpions today," Mack said.

Jamal hadn't noticed before that Mack's breath smelled of wine.

"What the meeting about?"

"I told them you were taking over the gang," Mack said. "They want to meet you."

"What they say when you told them that?"

"They say they want to vote for a new leader, but I told them that Randy said you was the new leader. They don't want to deal with that, then they got to deal with me," Mack said.

"What you got to do to get into the gang?" Tito asked.

"Jamal say you can be in it, you in it," Mack said.

Two girls came halfway down the stairs, stopped when they saw the three boys in the hallway, turned, and went back upstairs.

"So we go over to the clubhouse now so they can scope you," Mack said.

"Yeah, okay. You coming, Tito?"

"Yeah."

"Randy say I should be your warlord because, you know, when they's a fight or anything, I can really get down," Mack said.

"Okay."

"Bet!" Mack and Jamal exchanged fives, and then Mack and Tito.

"Let's go on over there," Mack said. "Yeah, and here the thing. Put it in your belt, man."

Jamal took the shiny pistol from Mack and put it in his belt.

CHAPTER EIGHT

Mack was the only one who talked on the way to the Scorpions clubhouse. When they passed some shops on 125th Street, Jamal saw their reflections in the windows. Tito was looking at him, and Jamal knew his friend was thinking about the gun. He was thinking about it too. It was heavy in his belt, and he kept touching it.

His legs were stiff as he walked. He felt that the gun was going to do something—fall out of his pants, or shoot all by itself.

The Scorpions used an old firehouse behind Marcus Garvey Park as their base. The firehouse had been boarded over and locked with chains, but there was a window in the back that could be reached by climbing a small ladder. Over the window there was a picture of a small gold shield with a black scorpion painted on it.

Mack went up first, then Tito, and then Jamal.

The Scorpions had brought a small television into the firehouse and some wooden chairs. They were sitting around it watching a kung fu movie. They didn't say anything when they saw Mack, Tito, and Jamal enter.

Jamal recognized most of the Scorpions.

"Yo, what it is?" Mack found a chair and sat in it. "What y'all watching?"

"This the dude that was supposed to take Bruce Lee's place," a guy Jamal knew as Angel said, nodding toward the Chinese karate fighter on the small screen. "But he ain't that tough."

"Yeah, yeah." Mack sat down on a box.

"Jamal, what's happenin'?" Angel spoke to Jamal without taking his eyes off the television.

"Everything's cool," Jamal said.

"Who your friend?"

"This is Tito." Jamal nodded toward Tito, then turned toward the Scorpions. "This is Blood, Terry, Indian, and Angel. I don't know this guy."

Tito nodded toward the Scorpions.

"This is Bobby Welcome," Mack said. "He's new."

"We been talking, man." Angel was thick-necked and wide-eyed. Jamal thought that if he drew him he could make him look like a horse. "Everybody ain't happy with Jamal taking over the Scorpions."

"You ain't happy?" There was a threat in Mack's voice.

"I didn't say I wasn't happy." Angel's voice rose. "I said *everybody* ain't happy, and I think we should talk on it."

"Yeah, well, you talk too much," Mack said.

Jamal felt his mouth go dry. He looked toward the television, where a guy was training by lifting heavy stones.

"Jamal ain't nothing but a kid," Indian said.

"He Randy's brother."

"That don't mean nothing." Blood took a long drink from his soda. Blood's throat moved up and down as he swallowed.

"We got to vote on it," Angel said.

"Who you vote for?" Jamal asked.

"I vote for Indian."

"Randy still the leader of the Scorpions," Mack said. "He just letting Jamal hold it for him until he get back in the world."

"Time he get out, my kids be in the Scorpions," Angel said.

"I don't like your mouth, man," Mack said. "You want to go down with me or something?"

"Ain't nobody want to go down with you," Indian said. He glanced toward Mack. "We just talking."

"Jamal ain't got no experience," Angel said. "He don't know how to handle the dealers, man. We gonna make some real money, he got to know how to deal with the dealers."

"You gonna talk that mess to Randy when his appeal go through?" Mack said.

"I'll talk it if I got to." Indian stood up and spread his legs. He had a narrow face, with thin slits for eyes.

"I got your back," Angel said.

Jamal wasn't sure what he should do. He thought about giving the gun to Mack. He stood and opened his coat and put his hand on it.

"He got a piece!" Blood was heavy and brown skinned, with light eyes. He was missing a tooth in the front of his mouth.

Indian looked at Jamal and took a step back.

"Why you think Randy want him to run the Scorpions?" Mack said. " 'Cause he know he don't go in for all this girl talk y'all be putting out. He put you to sleep faster than your mama did when you was little."

"I see he got the part, but I don't know if he got the heart," Indian said.

"Let it alone," Angel said to Indian.

"Why I got to let it alone?"

"His brother done already blow a dude away," Angel said. "That runs in the blood."

"What you say, Jamal?" Bobby Welcome said.

"Randy want me to be the head of the Scorpions, and I'm here," Jamal said.

"Sooner or later you got to go one-on-one," Indian said. "And you too young to take the strain."

"Ain't no one-on-one, fool," Mack said. "It's Jamal and Mack, and there ain't no turning back! You got a card, deal the sucker."

Indian looked over at Jamal, then turned away.

"Scotty say he need some legs tomorrow," Blood said. "He needs two guys. We going?"

"What you say, Jamal?" Mack asked. "We can use the money."

"Yeah."

"Who going?" Mack asked.

"Me and Indian," Blood said.

Mack looked over at Indian. "Yeah, that's cool. Just so long as certain people remember I got Jamal's back."

"He gonna be a Scorpion too?" Angel pointed toward Tito. "How old is he, six?"

"He be one if I say he be one," Jamal said.

"How old *you* is?" Mack asked Angel.

"Fourteen," Angel said. "Everybody else here is either fourteen, fifteen, or sixteen. He ain't but twelve, maybe even eleven."

"He don't got to be fourteen or nothing to deal," Indian said. "But being the leader of the Scorpions is something else."

On the screen one karate school was fighting against another one.

Jamal sat down and watched it for a while. He didn't look at Tito. If he looked at Tito, he might have seen that Tito was afraid, and his own fear would come out. He didn't want to see Tito being afraid, or even smiling. These guys, Indian, Mack, and Blood, weren't the kind of guys you did a lot of smiling around.

They watched the rest of the movie, then Blood said he had to split. Then Mack said he had to leave. Tito and Jamal started to go with him.

"Yo, Jamal!" Indian called to him.

"What?"

"I ain't got nothing against you or nothing," Indian said. "I just think you kind of young to be running the Scorpions."

"Yeah."

•

They left Mack on Morningside, across from St. Joseph's. As soon as Mack had crossed the street, Tito asked Jamal if he was afraid.

"No, man."

"Yes, you were."

"I look afraid?"

"No, but I know you were afraid," Tito said. "You going to stay the head of the Scorpions?"

"I don't know."

"They scared of Mack," Tito said.

"They scared of Mack and me, too, if I got the gun."

"I don't like that gun," Tito said as they started past the projects. "You going to keep it?"

"I don't know."

"You ever shoot a gun before?"

"What you think?"

"You want to go shoot it?"

"Where?"

"We can shoot it in Central Park. Down near the water."

"Tomorrow after school?"

"Yeah."

"Okay."

"You see them poles?"

85

"What poles?"

"The poles in the clubhouse. That used to be a firehouse."

"You mean those poles the guys slide down?"

"Yeah."

"We can try that."

"I could be a fireman," Tito said. "I could save people."

●

When Sassy was in the bathroom and Mama was at the store to put her numbers in, Jamal hid the gun in the sofa. He lifted the cushion and slid the gun between the arm of the chair and the seat.

He put the cushion back on just before Sassy opened the bathroom door.

"Mama tell you that Daddy was here?"

"He was?" Jamal shifted his weight to look as natural as he could. "What happened?"

"He came talking about if she need some money or anything," Sassy said. "Mama said she did, and he said that he was going to start some job and soon's he got some money he was gonna give her some."

"He always saying that."

"He getting skinny."

"What he say to you?" Jamal asked.

"Nothing, except how I was, stuff like that."

"What he say about me?"

"He said how come you ain't keeping the place cleaner."

"He said that?"

"Uh-huh. He said you should do the dishes every day because you got to take his place as man of the house."

Jamal smiled. He knew his father hadn't said that. "He tell you how cute you were?"

"He did mention it about once or twice, maybe three times," Sassy said.

"What he say about Randy?"

"Said he was going to get some money for Randy, too. He act like he was all broke up over Randy."

"He don't even care."

"I think he do."

"Why?"

" 'Cause he act like he do," Sassy said. "Randy his son, the same as you."

"How long he stay?"

"He coming back tonight," Sassy said. "He said he's going to bring something from McDonald's."

"I don't care if he do come back."

"Mama act like she wasn't glad to see him, but I think she was."

Jamal could barely remember when his father had lived with them. All he remembered was a few times when his father had taken him under one arm and Sassy under the other and run around the park outside the projects where they used to live. More than those few times, though, he remembered when his father had lost his job and sat around the house. He drank beer all the time at first, and then he switched to wine and started being nasty to Mama. Then one day Mama dressed Randy, him, and Sassy and left. Jamal remembered asking Mama what was wrong and her not answering. Jamal knew something was wrong. Her lip was swollen, and she was crying. Sassy had been crying too, because she had a cold. Randy wanted to go back to get his ball, and Mama kept begging for Randy to hurry.

They had gone to Mama's cousin's house, and they all slept on the floor that night. They stayed there for a few days, until Mama had found them another apartment.

At first Daddy used to come around a lot. Half the time he had been drinking. After a while he came around less and less. Jamal felt the same about his father as he did about Randy. They were both gone, and each of them had taken a little piece of Mama with them that they couldn't bring back.

●

"Can I go into your room?"

"You gonna draw out the window?"

"Yeah."

"For a quarter."

"I ain't giving you no quarter," Jamal said.

"Then I'm gonna take your picture when you done with it."

Jamal liked to draw the backyard from Sassy's window. It used to be filled with garbage that people had thrown from the windows. But when the old Chinese man who was the super of the building next door built a garden, people got together to keep the yard nice. They offered the old man money to help him with it, but he didn't take it. He just spent all of his time, or at least the time when he wasn't taking care of the building, working in the garden, making it nice.

Jamal began to sketch the small garden. He had sketched it at least thirty times, each time making it look a little better than he had the time before.

Sometimes when Jamal drew, he would look at things carefully and keep his mind on the drawing. Other times he wouldn't even think about what he was drawing. It was as if his pencil went by itself as he thought about other things.

Now he wasn't thinking about the garden. He was thinking about the Scorpions. He had been afraid. Tito knew it, and maybe even the other Scorpions knew it. Jamal knew they were afraid of Mack. Mack was sixteen and had already been in Spofford twice.

They were afraid of the gun, too. He remembered how Indian had stopped cold when he had seen the gun in Jamal's belt. Still, Jamal wasn't sure if he wanted to be a Scorpion or not. He didn't want to have to fight Indian. Indian was wild-looking, and Randy had told him once that when the Scorpions had had a fight in the Bronx it was Indian who had knocked a guy out with one punch. But maybe he wouldn't have to fight Indian. Not as long as he had the gun, anyway.

CHAPTER NINE

Jamal came out of Sassy's room when he heard
Mama come in. She was carrying some packages,
and Sassy took them from her and put them on the
table.

"Jevon here?" Mama asked.

"Unh-uh." Sassy shook her head.

The corners of Mama's mouth tightened for a moment, and then relaxed into a smile.

"Sassy, see if I got some red pepper in the cabinet," Mama said.

Sassy went to the cabinet and found the red pepper.

"What you making?"

"Devil fish," Mama said. "What you been doing,
Jamal?"

"Nothing. Daddy coming?"

"He said he was," Mama said, dragging out the
"said." "Lord knows what that man be doing half
the time."

The fish had already been cleaned, and Mama
washed it carefully and patted it dry. Then she dusted
it with flour and spread it on the chopping board.
Jamal counted six small fish.

"Mama, didn't Daddy say that Jamal should do all the dishes from now on?" Sassy asked.

"I ain't got time for no foolishness, girl," Mama said. "You got any homework?"

"I finished it in school."

"Jamal, how about you?"

"I ain't got none," Jamal said. He remembered that there had been homework on the board, but he had forgotten to copy it.

"Don't start any mess up when your daddy gets here," Mama said. She covered the fish with a clean dish towel. Then she put some lard in a frying pan and turned up the flame beneath the pan.

Jamal stood in the kitchen door, leaning against one side of the narrow frame, and watched the lard slowly move across the pan as it melted. Mama took a cup of chicken broth from the refrigerator and put it in another pot. She put black pepper, red pepper, and white pepper in the broth and stirred it gently as that, too, heated up.

"Is your room clean, Sassy?"

"Yes, unless Jamal messed it up. He was in there."

"I didn't mess up nothing," Jamal said.

"Both of you go in and check the living room."

Jamal let Sassy go in first, then remembered the gun in the couch, and went in quickly behind her.

The living room wasn't too bad, and Sassy picked up the few things that were out of place. She put the television on, with the sound down low so Mama wouldn't hear it and tell them to turn it off.

"You can have my fish," Sassy said.

"I don't want your fish," Jamal answered.

"You can have it anyway."

"Shut up."

•

Jevon Hicks knocked on the door at exactly six o'clock. Sassy opened it, and Jevon picked her up in his arms.

"Girl, you getting heavy!"

"Hi, Daddy."

"Sassy, ask your father if he wants to eat in the living room or in the kitchen."

"Anywhere the food is!" Jevon answered Mama's question.

"Hi, Daddy."

"How you doing, boy?"

"Okay."

"You been helping your mother around the house?" Jevon Hicks took off his topcoat and sat on the other end of the couch. He was wearing an old suit, but his shoes looked new.

"Yeah," Jamal said. "I been helping her."

"Daddy, tell Jamal he should do the dishes all the time."

"That ain't no man's job," Jevon said. "How you been doing in school?"

"Okay."

"Okay? That ain't good enough," Jevon said. "You can't take no 'okay' to the Man and expect to make a living."

"I'm doing good," Jamal said.

"Well, that's better. I know you don't want me to have to take my belt off and straighten you out."

Jamal looked away. He felt his eyes stinging with tears. He hated it when his father came and talked about "straightening him out." It wasn't like he was there all the time to talk to him or help or anything. Just when he came around once in a while he had to talk like he was so interested. He wished he was away in Puerto Rico or someplace, like Tito's father.

Jevon Hicks was talking to Sassy, telling her about some job he was supposed to start working for a dry cleaner. Jamal could smell the fish. He knew that Mama would fry it for about half a minute in the lard and then lay it in the broth with all the pepper. It was good that way, better than when she just fried it with cornmeal.

"Soon as I can spell *able* I'm going to try to get me some wheels," his father was saying at the kitchen table. "Maybe we can go out for a drive sometime. When the last time you been out to Coney Island?"

"I haven't been out to Coney Island since . . ." Mama looked up at the ceiling. "Since just before Mr. Lee died. You remember that man used to work out at the race track?"

"Old man, crippled back?"

"Yes."

"Let's go to Great Adventure," Sassy said.

"Too many accidents happening out there." Jevon Hicks took a fish from the platter. "Plus it take all day to get out there. I bet you use a tank of gas getting there and back."

"We got to see about Randy, too," Mama said.

"How much you say that lawyer want?" Jevon asked.

"He say he need two thousand dollars all together."

"I can come up with half of it in a few months, but I can't make the whole thing."

"The lawyer said he can start the appeal with five hundred dollars," Jamal said.

"That's what he tell your mama," his father answered. "Them lawyers will five-hundred-dollar you to death. You got to have the whole thing, and then you can say, 'Here's the money, get him out.'"

"You think he's going to get out, Jevon?" Mama asked.

"That ain't even the question. You can't tell what the Man gonna do unless you go to him. The question is what we going to do to get our blood out the jail."

"Nothing we can do except get the money," Jamal said.

"So what you doing about it?" his father asked.

"Me?"

"Yeah, you," his father said. "He your brother, ain't he?"

"Yeah."

"Well, it's about time you started acting like a man and started seeing what you can do about it."

"He can't get no job 'cause he's only twelve," Sassy said.

"When I was his age I had plenty of jobs. You can't get no job if you walk in and start talking about how you only twelve," his father said. "You don't want no job anyway. What you want to be is a mama's boy."

"He helps me out plenty around the house," Mama said. "Don't he, Sassy?"

"Yeah, Jamal helps Mama a lot," Sassy said.

"You still drawing them pictures?"

Jamal didn't answer. He knew his father didn't like his drawing.

"I think he probably better off just helping me take care of the house so I don't have to worry when I'm working," Mama said. "You know how the dope heads are around here."

"Randy even had trouble keeping a job," Sassy said.

"That's 'cause Randy don't take a whole lot of lip." Jevon Hicks took the last potato. "They don't want you around if you stand up for yourself. That's what Jamal got to learn."

•

His father stayed until eleven o'clock. Most of the time they watched television. Mama talked more than she usually did, and Jamal knew that she was happy having her husband home. When Jevon started acting restless, looking at the clock, they all knew he was going to leave. Mama got quiet. They all

95

did, waiting for him to say that he was going.

"What time is it?" he asked.

"It's not that late," Mama said. "You want some coffee?"

His father looked at his watch and mumbled something about having to get up early the next day.

He said good-bye to Sassy first, hugging her to his side.

"You got to act more like a young man," he said to Jamal.

"I know," Jamal said.

"How you know?" he asked.

"I'm the only man here, ain't I?"

"Don't get fresh, Jamal," Mama said. "Sometimes that boy gets so fresh."

Mama walked him to the door. Then he was gone. Later she asked Jamal to do the dishes, and he did.

He didn't know what it was, but it always felt the same when his father came to visit them. It didn't matter what they talked about or did, but when his father left, Jamal felt bad. It wasn't that he felt bad about his leaving, either. He was used to that. It was just little things his father said, mostly about Jamal not acting like a man. It was as if he was supposed to be doing something but didn't know what it was.

Mama said that sometimes when a man was broke up from his family it was hard for him to see them again because he felt he had failed them. Jamal could understand that. Sometimes when things were going bad for him and Mama and Sassy and he couldn't do anything about it, he just felt like walking away too. He could understand how his father felt, but it didn't help anything.

●

Jamal looked at the gun before he put it into his sneaker. "Sterling .380 D/A" was printed on the side of it, and he wondered what it meant. He tied the sneaker carefully and put it in a paper bag with its mate. That's how he took it to school. The gun seemed heavier than it had the day before.

The morning went okay. Mrs. Rich asked if anybody didn't have the homework, and he hadn't put his hand up. Then she told Christine to collect it, and she gave her the answers. While she was teaching decimals again, Christine marked the papers. She gave them out just before they left.

"Any problems that you got wrong go over tonight," Mrs. Rich said. "We're going to have a quiz either tomorrow or Monday."

Dwayne started up again. He started telling everybody how Jamal had punked out.

"Now I got to beat his butt twice." Dwayne was talking to some of the girls in the class. "Maybe I'll make him bring me a dollar a day to keep me off his butt."

Myrna gave Dwayne a disgusted look. She didn't like him any more than Jamal did.

"You be down in the storeroom at lunchtime or

I'm going to beat your butt right in the classroom," Dwayne said.

"I'll be there," Jamal said.

The girls started spreading the news that there was going to be a fight in the storeroom at noon. Jamal heard about it from one of the Davis twins.

"Why you going to fight him when you know you can't win?" she asked.

"I don't know that," Jamal said.

"You knew it when he beat your butt the other day," she said. There was a stupid look on her face. She was laughing at him. He looked right at her, but he was so mad he was almost crying.

Jamal had one more class before lunch. Instead of going to it, he went to the third floor and found Tito. He told Tito about the fight.

"You going to fight him?"

"You take the gun down to the storeroom," Jamal said. "Leave it in the bag and put it on the shelf. Okay?"

"I don't think you should shoot nobody," Tito said.

"I ain't going to shoot him."

"What you going to do?"

"Just take the gun down there like I said," Jamal said.

"No."

"Why?"

" 'Cause I don't want you to shoot nobody."

"I'm just going to scare him," Jamal said.

"I don't think you should take the gun," Tito said. He looked down at the floor and twisted the toe of his sneaker at a place where the floor was cracked.

"Okay, then I'm going to go down there and get beat up," Jamal said. "I'm going to stand right there and get beat up and say my friend Tito wants me to get beat up."

Tito looked up at Jamal, half shrugged, then looked down at the floor again. "Maybe you should give the gun back to Mack," Tito said.

"Okay, I'll give it back to him this afternoon," Jamal said.

"Promise?"

"After we shoot it."

"Okay."

"You going to take it down to the storeroom?"

"Yeah." Tito nodded and took the gun.

•

"Jamal, where were you?" Mr. Hunter asked.

"I got a real bad upset stomach," Jamal said. "I had to go to the bathroom."

Mr. Hunter took a breath, and his shoulders seemed to rise as he tried to think of something to say. Then they went down, and he went on with the class.

Dwayne was saying something to Billy and looking back at Jamal. Dwayne was acting as if he couldn't control the way he was laughing.

Indian was a lot tougher than Dwayne, Jamal thought. Indian looked as tough as Mack, but maybe smarter. Guys who were tough seemed tougher when they weren't too smart, and Mack didn't seem too smart.

Indian was tough, but he had shut up when he saw the gun in Jamal's belt. Dwayne was going to shut up too. Jamal could imagine him with his slanty-looking face coming into the storeroom and grinning and talking about how bad he was and everything. Then he'd see the gun and he'd know that he'd better shut up. He would shut up too. Just like Indian.

The bell rang and the class started back to its homeroom.

"Hey, Dwayne." Billy was close to Jamal. "I bet you can't knock him out."

"I bet I can," Dwayne said.

"What you say, Jamal?" Billy cupped his hand as if he were holding a microphone, and put it in front of Jamal.

"We see what go down," Jamal said.

Dwayne pushed him against the wall.

"What you say, fool?"

"I see you in the storeroom," Jamal said. "That's what I said."

Jamal turned and walked to his homeroom. He thought maybe he should just go on and fight Dwayne. He wasn't scared of him. Even if he lost it didn't make any difference to Jamal, because you couldn't get hurt that much in a fight with just fists.

But then, he thought, if he fought him and he got beat up bad, then maybe Dwayne would try to take the gun. No, that wouldn't do. He thought about that a little bit, but he thought even more about Dwayne laughing at him. That wasn't right, Dwayne laughing at people.

CHAPTER TEN

"Then I ain't going in," Jamal said.

"He punking out!"

"I ought to slap your face right here." Dwayne stood as close as he could to Jamal, looking down at him.

"Look how scared he look." Tamia Davis was trying to look around Dwayne's shoulder to see Jamal.

"You want to fight me, then just you and me got to go in," Jamal said.

"I paid two dollars for my ticket!" Billy said. "You know I got to see it."

"You real bad, now you hiding behind Dwayne, huh?" Jamal spit the words out at Billy Ware, then started to push past Dwayne and down the hall. Dwayne grabbed him by the arm and spun him around.

"You punking out?"

"You the one don't want to go in without all your friends," Jamal said.

"Go on in." Billy waved his hand toward the storeroom. "We just stay out here and listen to it."

"I want to see it."

Jamal glanced over to where Tamia Davis leaned against the wall.

"Come on!" Dwayne turned and went into the storeroom.

Jamal looked at the grinning faces around him, and his mouth went dry. Tito was standing near the back of the crowd. Jamal wanted to tell Tito to keep the rest of the kids out, but the words didn't come.

He wasn't afraid of Dwayne, he told himself. He wasn't even afraid of being beaten up by Dwayne.

The inside of the storeroom was musty. It wasn't used for supplies anymore. The only things in it now were some old maps, dusty and rolled in the corner, and books that the school had used years before. The room was too small to be used as a classroom, so it was used mostly by older kids sneaking a smoke, because it could be locked from the inside and because the small window could be opened to let the smoke out.

It was Jamal who turned the latch.

"Why you lock the door, punk?"

Dwayne had pushed himself up against Jamal so that their chests were just touching. Dwayne wasn't that sure of himself, Jamal thought, or he would have just started the fighting instead of wolfing at him.

Jamal pushed Dwayne away from him, and Dwayne threw a punch that caught him squarely in the nose and sent him backward against the door.

For a moment Jamal's head spun, and before he could get it clear, Dwayne hit him again. He reached out blindly for Dwayne's body, felt another blow to his face, and then grabbed one of Dwayne's arms.

He held on as best as he could while Dwayne kept punching him in the back of his head. He tried to lift one of Dwayne's legs and throw him down the way he had on the street, but Dwayne stepped around him and punched him in the back.

Jamal stepped back quickly and got his hands up.

Dwayne came at him again, bobbing and weaving like a boxer.

"You ain't so bad now, huh?" Dwayne's face was screwed up in anger.

He came charging in, and Jamal threw a kick that caught him on the leg. Dwayne spun around in a karate move and Jamal caught the kick in his stomach.

All the air went out of Jamal, and his legs buckled. He thought he was going to throw up as he staggered backward. Dwayne came at him again and started to throw a flying kick, but slipped as his leg went up. He went sprawling across the floor and landed hard on his shoulder.

Jamal looked around. He saw the paper bag on the shelf just above where Dwayne was. He went toward Dwayne, and Dwayne kicked him in the leg. He fell down on top of Dwayne, throwing a punch that missed as he did. Dwayne rolled over twice and sprang to his feet. He assumed a karate stance again.

Dwayne didn't know any karate. Jamal knew that—he had just been lucky with the kick. But Jamal's face felt as if it were swelling from the punch in the nose, and when he wiped his mouth there was blood on his fingers.

Dwayne was at him again and started another kick. Jamal jumped at Dwayne, caught the kick on the side of his leg, and grabbed Dwayne's head. He twisted it and tried to throw Dwayne down, but this time it was Dwayne who grabbed Jamal's leg and lifted him up.

Jamal felt himself leave the ground and start to fall backward. He reached out to grab Dwayne, caught his shirt for a moment, then felt himself falling. Dwayne punched at him as he fell to the floor, then backed away. Jamal saw that he had ripped Dwayne's shirt.

Jamal got up quickly. Dwayne was taking off the ripped shirt.

"You paying for this, sucker!" Dwayne was breathing hard.

Jamal reached up and found the bag. He took it down and pulled out the gun.

Dwayne was in front of the window, and Jamal couldn't see his face too clearly. He lifted the gun and pointed it at him.

"That ain't real," Dwayne said.

"Come on," Jamal said. There was the taste of

blood in his mouth. "You gonna see it's real."

Dwayne didn't move.

Jamal held the gun pointed at Dwayne. He could hear the sound of his own breathing and Dwayne's even heavier breathing. Dwayne was getting out of breath. Jamal thought he still had a chance to win the fight.

"That ain't nothing but a cap pistol," Dwayne said.

"Come on and find out," Jamal said.

Dwayne straightened up and looked at Jamal.

"I know it ain't real."

"The Scorpions don't have no fake guns," Jamal said.

"You ain't no Scorpion."

"I'm the leader of the Scorpions."

There was a banging on the door and Billy's voice saying that he wanted to come in.

Jamal took a step toward Dwayne, lifting the gun toward his face.

"Hey, Jamal . . ." Dwayne's voice cracked as he spoke.

Dwayne started backing up. He put his hands in front of his chest. Jamal was trembling. His heart was racing. He looked at Dwayne's face and saw his fear. He moved closer to Dwayne and watched the bigger boy lift his hands until they were in front of his face and slide down the wall to the floor.

Jamal kicked Dwayne on his leg. Once, twice,

harder and harder. Dwayne kept his hands over his head.

"Please!" He was wrapping himself into a ball.

Jamal kicked him in the side, hurting his toe. He started to kick him with the other foot, then stopped.

"Next time you dead, man," he said. He backed away, found the bag on the floor, and put the gun in it. He looked back at Dwayne, still in the corner, now crying. He turned away.

Billy and the others were still around the outside of the storeroom.

"His face bleedin'!" Tamia Davis giggled.

Jamal pushed through the small knot of kids and started for the stairway.

His leg was hurting, and he stumbled as he went down the stairs.

"Jamal!" Tito's voice behind him.

Jamal didn't stop. He was crying now. He went through some more kids entering the lunchroom, and through the door to the school yard.

"You have a pass?" a lower-grade teacher called after him.

Jamal kept going. Through the school yard and onto the avenue.

Jamal wasn't sure why he headed toward the boat basin. He hadn't even noticed how cold it was until he had passed 96th Street.

He thought about Dwayne. What would he say? Maybe he would go to Mr. Davidson and tell him that Jamal had a gun. Jamal told himself that he didn't care.

Jamal thought about not going home, about never going home again. He would just stay on the street. Maybe he would go to Chicago or someplace like that. Maybe even California.

He was crying. It was Dwayne's fault. All of it. Now he would have to go away and never see Mama or Sassy again. No, he would see them again. Maybe he would wait until Randy got out of jail before he came back. Then he would come back too, and they wouldn't even recognize him. He'd have a suit on, a white shirt, and a tie.

A class of schoolchildren was in the park. They were playing soccer, with the boys against the girls. Jamal watched them for a while. The girls were doing okay against the boys. Jamal thought that it was probably because the boys weren't that good.

The wind picked up, and he shivered. He thought about going home. He needed his coat. The police would probably be at the school, so he couldn't get his jacket. He had an old jacket at home. Maybe he could sneak in when nobody was around. He would leave a note.

He started thinking about what would be in the note, and he began to cry again. He didn't want to leave home. He didn't know what else to do, though. He had heard about what happened in jail and in youth houses. The big guys ganged up on you and beat you up and then they had sex with you.

He was shaking. A young man was passing by, saw Jamal, and hurried his step.

He hadn't killed anybody. Maybe he wouldn't have to go to jail. Maybe he would just get probation or something like that. Maybe even a warning. Mr. Davidson would put him out of school, and he would have to get a job.

A pile of dead leaves had blown into the walkway, and he crunched them underfoot as he walked.

He didn't know what to do with the gun. He thought about throwing it away. But if the police came and got him, they would make him take them to the place he threw it away.

Things were just so messed up. He had gone out of the house in the morning and things hadn't been so bad, and now they were. Had Randy thought the same thing? Had he stood outside the store and thought that it would be easy and that he would get the money? Then something happened and a man was dead, and his whole life was thrown away.

The fight with Dwayne kept coming into Jamal's mind. He imagined himself in the storeroom again and again. He couldn't beat Dwayne. Dwayne was older than he was and stronger. Even if he could get some good punches in, Dwayne would still win. Dwayne just thought he was so bad. He hadn't been so bad when he saw the gun was real. Indian had backed off when he saw the gun. People didn't mess with you when you had a gun. Maybe it wasn't right to have it, but people still didn't mess with you.

It was getting colder. An old man and a woman walked arm in arm, holding their coats closed at the neck. He thought about going down to 42nd Street. What he wanted to do was find a mirror and see how he looked. He knew he could go to The Deuce and find a bathroom down there.

Two women walked out onto the finger pier and stopped at a boat. They were dressed alike. Both of them had on what looked like jogging suits. One of the women carried a large, white shopping bag.

Jamal wished that he had a boat. He wished he knew the two women. If he knew them, everything in his life would be different. He would probably have a boat, and they would ask him for a ride. He wouldn't even know Dwayne. He would probably be finished school with a diploma and know a lot of places to go with the boat.

The two women got on one of the boats and went into the little compartment. Jamal thought about what they would be doing in there. He thought they would be talking about the president, or maybe about going for a ride in the boat.

In front of him two teenagers passed. One of them looked Spanish. His hair was cut short on the sides, with a tail.

The other one was either Spanish or just plain black. They stopped near the railing and looked over at the boats. The black guy looked over at him. Jamal reached into the bag and put his hand on the gun. The two teenagers started on.

He decided to go to The Deuce. He got up and started walking downtown, when he thought he heard somebody call his name. At first he didn't think it was real, but then he turned around and saw Tito waving his arm.

CHAPTER ELEVEN

"How come you down here?"

"I saw you going out the school—Dwayne's talking about how you're a Scorpion. You told him?"

Jamal looked at Tito. "What else he say?"

"He said you were going to shoot him," Tito said. "What you doing now?"

"Everybody know about it?"

"Mostly the kids hanging around the storeroom. You won the fight or he won it?"

"He won it, I guess," Jamal said. "He said I had the gun in the storeroom?"

"Yeah, he was real scared when you left," Tito said. "Everybody said you beat him up, but I saw the way you looked when you came out of the storeroom."

"How you know I was down here?"

"This is where we come sometimes," Tito said. "I went by your house and nobody was home."

"You left school early?"

"Yeah." Tito smiled.

"What you think is going to happen now?"

"If Dwayne tell the teachers you had the gun in school, you're going to be in real trouble."

"I was thinking of running away."

"Everybody was talking about how they didn't know how tough you were and how they didn't know you were a Scorpion," Tito said. He was walking with his head down. "Everybody except Tamia."

"What she say?"

"She said you ain't no Scorpion."

"What you think I should do?"

"You scared to go home?"

"I ain't scared," Jamal said.

"Go home."

"You want to keep the gun?"

"In my house?" Tito looked surprised.

"Yeah."

"You want to shoot it?"

"No, man," Jamal shook his head. "I almost shot Dwayne."

"You were going to kill him?"

"If he . . ."

Tito jerked his head away and looked out over the river. Jamal had seen him do that before. When things were bad, or when Jamal said things that Tito didn't want to hear, he would do that, jerk his head away so that Jamal couldn't see his face.

"I didn't even point the gun at him," Jamal said, knowing that Tito wouldn't believe him.

Tito didn't turn around.

On the river a barge drifted by, towed by a black-and-red tugboat. Gulls screeched noisily as they circled over the barge. Jamal could see someone standing in the wheelhouse of the boat. It looked like a woman. He watched her for a while as she stood motionless, and then he turned back to Tito.

"You didn't think I was going to shoot nobody, right?"

"You want to throw the gun away?"

"I think we should give it back to Mack," Jamal said.

"Suppose Dwayne tells Mr. Davidson?" Tito asked.

"You think he's gonna tell?"

"Unh-uh."

"You gonna keep it at your house?" Jamal asked.

"You want to shoot it first?"

"Okay."

It was getting darker. The air felt crisp, almost tingly. Jamal thought it might rain. They walked downtown until they got to the entrance of the park.

There was a flight of stairs that went down into the park and led to a path that went for a way along the wall that edged the park. Tito and Jamal stopped alongside of the path, at the foot of the steps.

"You want to shoot it?" Jamal asked.

"Yeah."

"Go ahead," Jamal said. "You have to pull this thing up; then you can shoot it."

Tito looked around, then down at the pistol, which Jamal handed him.

"It's heavy," he said.

"Go on, shoot it."

Tito held the gun at arm's length, squeezed his

eyes almost shut, and pulled the trigger. Nothing happened. Then he put both hands on the trigger and pulled again.

The gun went off and jerked upward in Tito's hand. He looked at Jamal wide-eyed.

"Put it back in the bag," Jamal said.

Tito quickly put the gun back into the bag.

"Oh, mess, she saw us!"

Tito turned and saw a thin woman standing near a lamppost. There was a small, white dog on the end of the leash she held. Her face was very white, and she didn't move.

"Come on." Tito pulled Jamal by the arm.

Jamal ran up the stairs behind Tito, stopping only once, to turn to see the woman again. She was still frozen to the spot where they had first seen her.

•

"Mama, how you spell *secretary*?" Sassy asked.

"How you going to be a secretary if you can't even spell it?" Mama asked.

"I ain't going to be no secretary," Sassy said. "I'm just going to be like a student secretary or something. They just want to find out what I want to be."

"You ain't going to get no job no matter what you do, cause you ain't old enough," Jamal said.

"She old enough to wear her jacket home from school," Mama said. "And you still ain't told me why Tito come here with your jacket this afternoon, as cold as it was outside."

"We were just fooling around," Jamal said.

"And why wasn't you hungry this evening?"

"Just wasn't."

"And why you puffy around the eye?"

"Told you I got in a fight," Jamal said.

"Uh-huh. Well, it sure must have been some fight, if you had to leave your jacket in school," Mama said.

"If Sassy would keep her big mouth shut sometimes, everything would be okay," Jamal said.

"Sassy just trying to be family," Mama said. "You sure can't fault her for that."

•

Jamal had arrived home at six thirty, and Sassy had already told Mama about Tito's bringing his coat home. But the thing that worried him most was what Dwayne had said in school. If he had told Mr. Davidson about the gun, Jamal was sure Mr. Davidson would call the police.

Every step outside the apartment, every footstep in the hallway, sounded like the police. His stomach was in a tight knot. Mama had said that she had gone to a different bodega on the avenue to buy some plantains, and that the guy who owned it, Mr. Gonzalez, said he needed someone to help out in the afternoons.

"You go around there," she had said. "You might get lucky."

Jamal had nodded, and said that he would go after school. Mama looked at him and asked if anything was wrong. Jamal said no, but he knew Mama didn't believe him.

He didn't sleep well. There were noises going on in the hall all night. He remembered when the police had come for Randy. They had all been asleep. Randy was on the couch, and Jamal was sleeping with Sassy. They heard this banging on the door, and he had come out to see what was going on. Mama was already standing in the middle of the floor. Jamal looked in the direction that Mama was looking, and he saw Randy standing in the middle of the floor. He had put his pants on and was hurrying into his sneakers.

Mama hadn't said anything; she just looked at Randy. Jamal didn't know what was going on, but he knew it had to do with Randy.

The banging on the door had started again, and somebody yelled for them to open the door, that it was the police. Still Mama hadn't moved. Randy had his sneakers on and then asked Mama if she had any money.

Mama didn't say anything. It was like she knew that the police were coming to get Randy. It was part of living on the block, part of walking past Mr. Evans's raggedy store, part of what their lives were about. If you were a part of the life they were living, Jamal thought, then after a while you did something and the police came and got you.

Randy had turned and gone to the window and opened it.

There was a loud cracking sound from the door, and it splintered away from the frame. A moment later two policemen in uniform and two other guys burst into the room. They had their guns out, pointing them around the room.

"There he goes!" a black cop said. He ran to the window, stuck the gun out, and started calling for Randy to come back into the room. When Randy came back into the room, he had lost one of his sneakers. That was how they had taken him away, with just his pants and one sneaker on.

●

Morning. There was a roach in the cornflakes. Jamal tried to think back to the last time he had put out some roach stuff. He had to do it again.

"Why roaches always be around poor people?" Sassy asked.

"Rich people get as many roaches as poor people," Mama said. "Anybody can get roaches in they house. They got roaches down on Park Avenue. Rats, too."

"All you see is roaches in poor people's houses," Sassy said, sticking to her point.

"You going to eat the cornflakes?" Jamal said.

"Not with no roaches in it!"

"Throw that box away," Mama said. "Make yourself some toast, honey."

"Jamal got that raisin bread yesterday," Sassy said. When she smiled, it was easier to see her dimple. "Those raisins look like roaches to me."

"You look like a roach to me," Jamal said.

"Jamal Hicks, how you fix your mouth to talk to your sister like that?"

"That's 'cause he's ignorant!" Sassy said. "You can always tell an ignorant child by the stupid stuff he be saying."

"You the one ignorant," Jamal said.

"Jamal, you going over to see about that job with Mr. Gonzalez?" Mama asked. "You could make some spending money for yourself."

"I'll go over there right after school."

●

Darnell was in Mr. Perry's class. Standing in the hallway, his cap at an angle on the back of his head, he was the first person to meet Jamal in school.

"Do you have or do you not have a gun?" Darnell asked.

"I ain't got no gun," Jamal said.

"That's what I told everybody," Darnell said. "Dwayne just got shamed 'cause you kicked his butt."

"He said I had a gun?"

"Yep!"

"He lyin'."

"You in the Scorpions?" Darnell asked.

"Who you, the F.B.I.?"

"No, man, I'm Harlem Vice, I'm Harlem Vice, and we so bad we got to say it twice!"

Jamal walked away from Darnell.

In Mrs. Rich's class Tamia asked him if he shot at Dwayne, and Jamal said no, he hadn't. Dwayne didn't say anything to him. He didn't even look at him.

Jamal wished he knew what Dwayne had told everybody, and whom he had told. At recess he saw Dwayne talking to Jerry Whaley and wondered if he was going to get Jerry to start something with him. Jerry was the roughest kid in school. He had been in the youth house two times and had stabbed a guy. Jamal knew they were talking about him because Jerry turned and looked in his direction.

It was a faculty day, which meant there was only a half day of school. No one mentioned the gun except Darnell and Tamia. No one mentioned Dwayne, either, until they reached Mrs. Mitchell's homeroom class. That's when Christian came over and said that Dwayne wanted to meet him outside.

"You going to fight him again?" Christian asked.

"He want to fight, I got to fight," Jamal said.

For the first time Jamal felt afraid of Dwayne. He wasn't sure what had changed, or why he was afraid of Dwayne, but he was. He felt his heart beating faster and his mouth dry up. He thought about the fight of the day before. Maybe he knew he couldn't beat Dwayne. But that hadn't mattered before. He wondered if Dwayne had a gun too.

Tito was waiting outside the homeroom. He wanted Jamal to come to his house. Jamal told him about meeting Dwayne.

"What are you going to do?"

"I don't know," Jamal said. "He might have Jerry Whaley with him."

"He's going to fight you too?"

"I don't know."

"I'll fight on your side," Tito said.

"You can't fight."

"So?"

"If they both jump on me, I'm going to mess them up."

"How?"

"I don't know."

●

Billy Ware was waiting on the corner with Dwayne. Jerry Whaley wasn't around. Tamia and her sister were there too. So was Darnell.

"What you want?" Jamal asked.

"I thinking about going to the police and telling them you got a gun," Dwayne said.

Jamal turned around. He breathed slowly through his mouth.

"I'm serious, too," Dwayne said.

Jamal knew Dwayne was serious, but he also knew he wasn't sure of himself again. If he had known what to do, if he had been really sure about going to the police, he would just have gone.

"You got to mess with the Scorpions, right?" Jamal said.

"I'm just messing with you," Dwayne said. He shifted from one foot to the other.

"You do what you got to do," Jamal said. "But you better know what you being about."

Jamal pivoted and started walking away.

"Here he come!" Darnell called out.

Jamal turned, but Dwayne hadn't moved.

●

"I don't know your mother." Mr. Gonzalez was turning jars of *recaito* on the shelves so that the labels all faced out.

"Yeah, you know her," Jamal said. "She come around here yesterday and bought some plantains."

"She's a big lady?"

"Yeah. She said you got a job helping out around the store."

"You a good boy?"

Jamal smiled. He looked at Mr. Gonzalez and saw that the old man was serious.

"Yeah, I'm okay," he said.

"Then I'll give you a try," Mr. Gonzalez said, putting his hand on Jamal's shoulder.

CHAPTER TWELVE

Jamal's first day was Saturday. He had to deliver packages and help in the store from ten in the morning until one in the afternoon.

"I'll give you fifteen dollars," Mr. Gonzalez had said. "And you can make some money on tips. But you got to be nice to people. Don't have a fresh mouth."

Jamal divided fifteen into two thousand. It came to a hundred and thirty-three. If he only worked on Saturdays, it would take him over two years to get the money to get Randy out.

"Suppose you work every day," Sassy said. "How long would it take you?"

"Mr. Gonzalez don't need nobody every day," Mama said. "Jamal be doing okay if he just help us out some."

Jamal thought about other things he could do with two thousand dollars. One thing he could do was buy a car. He couldn't get a new car, but he could get a used car.

"Mama, can you drive?"

"Sure I can drive," Mama said.

"If I got the whole two thousand dollars, we could buy a car," Jamal said.

"What we need a car for?" Mama asked.

Jamal shrugged. The thought of having a car made him smile. Maybe he couldn't get a new car, but he could get a nearly new car. He imagined himself driving it. In two years he would be fourteen and still couldn't get a license, but he could let Mama drive it and he could sit up front with her and let Sassy sit in the back. Maybe they could go upstate in the car to see Randy. Randy would look out the window and see him sitting in the car. He would be sitting in the driver's seat too.

•

He carried two boxes of groceries between ten and ten thirty. The first lady gave him a quarter, and the man, an old man who was thin and walked with a cane, gave him a dollar. When he wasn't carrying groceries, Mr. Gonzalez had him bring boxes of canned foods from the basement and put them on the shelves.

It felt good having a job. When people came into the store, they asked him questions. Things like where the bread was, or how much a package of franks cost. He didn't know all the answers, but he knew some of them, and it made him feel good to be the one people asked.

Not too many people wanted their groceries delivered. One woman had bought a whole box of heavy stuff that she wanted carried home with her, and Jamal thought he was going to drop it before he got it to her house.

He had tried to carry the box on his shoulder, but it hurt his shoulder. Then he tried to carry it on his head like he had seen some African dudes do on television, but that was even worse. It hurt his head something terrible, and his arms got tired from just holding the package up. He didn't say anything because he didn't want to lose the job.

"You're the weakest boy I have ever seen in my life." The woman, dark skinned with a lot of makeup on, wiped the perspiration that ran down the side of her face. "You into that dope?"

"No, ma'am."

"Well, why you so weak?"

"I'm not that weak," Jamal said, trying to walk straighter.

They reached the woman's apartment building on 123rd Street, and Jamal looked up to see a four-story building.

"You got a elevator in this building?"

"Why? Are you lazy or something?"

"I just asked."

The lady didn't say anything but walked down the hallway and started walking up the stairs. Jamal followed.

The stairs were really hard. The first time he had to go up a long flight of stairs, he almost dropped

125

the package twice. Now he had a new technique. He went up as fast as he could for five steps and then put the box down. Then he would rest a moment and do it all over again.

"If my food goes bad you're going to have to pay for it," the woman said.

"Yes, ma'am."

The woman lived on the fourth floor and had Jamal put the box on the kitchen table. Then she took a jar of change off the stove and shook out a coin.

"A dime?" Jamal looked at the coin.

"You don't want it?"

Jamal took the dime and started to leave.

"And when I see Mr. Gonzalez, I'm going to tell him to fire you because you're too weak."

Jamal shook his head and shrugged. "Yes, ma'am."

"Come on back here, boy," the woman said. She got the change jar again and shook out coins until she had reached a dollar, then gave it to Jamal.

"Thank you." Jamal smiled.

"Oh, you can show your teeth now, huh?"

Jamal started down the stairs as quickly as he could. The woman was right—he was kind of weak. Carrying all these packages would make him a lot stronger, though.

By noon all the deliveries had been finished, and all he was doing was getting everything in the store straight. Mr. Gonzalez had a lot of his friends come to the store. Most of the time they sat around and played dominoes. Whenever they wanted anything, Jamal had to go get it. Mr. Gonzalez didn't even want to wait on customers. Jamal waited on them. That was the best part of the job.

"Hey, you work here?" Jamal was putting boxes of spaghetti on the shelves. He looked down and saw Blood. He was wearing his Scorpion colors.

Yeah, sometimes," Jamal said.

"I didn't know you had a job," Blood said. "That's pretty hip."

"Ain't nothing to it," Jamal said. "What you want?"

"Give me a Slim Jim and a pack of Kools," Blood said.

Jamal took the Slim Jim from the box on the counter and the cigarettes from the rack behind the counter. He looked over toward Mr. Gonzalez to see if he was looking. He wasn't.

"That's a dollar seventy," Jamal said.

"I got to tell Indian you working here," Blood said, putting two dollars on the counter. "He been looking for you."

"What he looking for me for?"

"You find out when he find your narrow butt."

Blood took the wrapper off the Slim Jim and threw it on the counter. He picked up his change and the cigarettes and walked away.

Jamal swallowed hard. Mr. Gonzalez was still

playing dominoes. He hadn't noticed Blood in the store. Jamal figured that once Indian found out that he worked in the bodega, there would be trouble.

•

Tito came to the house Sunday after church. Sassy was in the street, and Mama was sitting in the window talking to Mrs. Bellinger, in the street below.

"Jamal, here comes Tito," Mama said. "He looking like something somebody done threw away."

Jamal squeezed into the space between Mama and the window frame and saw Tito on his way down the street. Tito was walking along near the building, head down.

"I'm going downstairs," Jamal said.

"Not in your suit you ain't!" Mama said.

"I won't get it messed up."

"I know, because you ain't going out in it," Mama said.

Jamal went into Sassy's room, got his clothes out of the bottom drawer, and started changing. He put on his old pants and sneakers, remembered that Mama wouldn't let him go out on Sundays with his sneakers on, and started looking for his school shoes. He had on one shoe and was just about to put the other one on when Tito knocked on the door.

"What's the matter?" Jamal whispered.

"Abuela found the gun."

"Man!" Jamal took a deep breath. "What she say?"

"She told me to get out." Tito's eyes were red

rimmed. "She said she wasn't even going to pray for me."

"Where the gun now?"

"Jamal?" Mama pulled herself in from the window. "What's wrong with Tito?"

"Nothing."

"Nothing my eye!" Mama sat in the overstuffed chair. "Tito, come on over here, child."

Tito didn't move. Mama put her hands on the arms of the chair and pushed herself up. She went over to where Tito stood facing the wall near Sassy's room. She put her arms around him and hugged him to her.

"What's wrong, baby? Now, you know you can tell me," Mama said.

"Abuela told me to leave and not to come back again," Tito said.

"She told you what?"

"She told me"—Tito's body was shaking—". . . don't come back again."

"Jamal, you got anything to do with this?" Mama asked.

"No, I was home."

"Tito, honey, look. Sometimes . . . Come on over here to the window so I can take a look at you."

Mama took Tito's hand and brought him over to the chair. She sat down in it and pulled him so he half sat, half leaned against her.

"Tito, sometimes we women got to be harder on

you young boys than we want to be. You know that and I know that. Me and your grandmother, we try our best, but God knows it's hard. We say things we don't mean because to say the things we mean is just too hurtin'. You be all right, 'cause that woman loves you as much as she loves life."

Jamal shifted his weight from one foot to the other.

"You want me to walk him home?" he asked Mama.

"What did you do, child?"

"Nothing."

"Yeah, well, if it's bad enough for your grandmother to put you out, I guess you don't want to tell me about it either."

Jamal saw Mama look at Tito's eyes, then get real close with a smile on her face so he wouldn't notice she was smelling his breath.

"Jamal, you hungry?" Mama winked at Jamal.

"No, ma'am."

"Boy, you ain't got a bit of . . . Well, you got to eat something anyway," Mama said. "Sit down at the table while I fix you and Tito a plate."

Jamal and Tito sat down at the table. Jamal kept looking at Tito. Tito kept looking down.

In his mind Jamal was begging Tito not to tell Mama about Abuela's finding the gun.

Mama made two plates of ox tails, snap beans, boiled potatoes, and pan gravy.

Sassy came home and saw Tito, and saw that he had been crying.

"What's wrong with you?" she asked.

"Watch your mouth," Mama said.

After they had eaten, Mama asked Tito if he wanted her to go home with him. He said no, and she told Jamal to go with him.

"And don't you worry, honey," Mama said. "That woman is going to be glad to see you, because she loves you. That don't mean she ain't going to be mad at you for whatever it was you did, but she still loves you. If she didn't love you, she wouldn't have no reason to be mad at you."

●

"You think she called the police?"

Tito shrugged.

"We got to get the gun back," Jamal said.

"Maybe she threw it away," Tito said.

"You told her where I got it from?"

"No."

"What you tell her?"

"I said I found it in school," Tito said.

"You told her it was you that had the gun?"

"Yeah."

"Man. . . ."

"She started talking in Spanish and everything," Tito said. "Then she started praying, and then she just told me to go away and never come back again. She said she didn't—"

131

Tito was crying again.

"Where the gun?"

"In the refrigerator."

"In the refrigerator? Why she put it there?"

"I don't know. She held it like it was a snake or something like that. You know, like she don't want to touch it."

"Why don't you tell her you want to throw it away?" Jamal said.

"I don't want to say anything to her."

"How come?"

"She was crying," Tito said. "I don't like to see her cry, Jamal. When she cry, she looks so different. That makes all my insides start to cry and everything. Then I feel so bad."

"Tito, we got to get the gun," Jamal said. "If she take it to the police or something, then maybe we got to . . . I don't know."

"What you want to do?"

"Get the gun."

"You can't hurt . . . I won't let you hurt Abuela."

"I'm not going to. How you figure I'm gonna hurt her?" Jamal said angrily. "How you figure that?"

They got to Tito's house and went quietly up the stairs. Tito was crying again.

"Jamal, I don't have the key."

Jamal shrugged. "Maybe I'll tell her that I got a friend who's a cop and I can give it to him, and then he'll do something with it and everything will be okay."

"How you going to tell her that?" Tito asked. "She going to know you're not telling the truth."

"What else we gonna do?"

"That gun is too much trouble."

They got to Tito's landing and Tito sat on the floor outside his door. Jamal didn't say anything. He just waited for Tito to be all right.

Tito didn't move for a long time. Jamal went to the door and pushed it gently.

"Tito!" he whispered hoarsely.

Tito looked at him and saw that the door was open.

Tito went to the door and opened it quietly. He went in and looked around. Jamal was right behind him. Abuela was nowhere in sight.

"Maybe she went out," Jamal whispered.

Tito went to her room and saw that the door was closed. He put his ear against the door. Then he made a sign to Jamal. Abuela was in the room, praying.

Jamal went to the refrigerator. He opened the door. There was the gun, next to a covered plate. He picked it up. It was cold, and now seemed even heavier than before. He put it in his pocket.

He went to the door. In a moment he was in the hallway and headed for the stairs. He stopped, and turned back to where Tito's eyes still stared at him from behind the slightly ajar door.

Jamal went back and opened the door. He took Tito's hand in his and held it for a while.

"Go on, Jamal!" Tito pleaded. "Before she comes out."

"You're my best friend in the whole world, Tito," Jamal said.

He left. He wanted to say more, but he couldn't -think of anything to say.

Long before he got to St. Nicholas Avenue, he told himself that the only thing to do was to throw the gun away. But already part of him knew that he wasn't going to do it.

CHAPTER THIRTEEN

There hadn't been one question that Jamal was sure about on the social studies test. It was all about the War of 1812 and the French and Indian Wars. He had remembered, vaguely, Mr. Hunter talking about those wars, but they hadn't sounded very interesting. He wasn't the only one who had them all wrong. Christian had them all wrong, too. That's why he and Christian were in Mr. Davidson's office. Oswaldo Vazquez was there, too.

"What did you do?" Christian asked.

"I threw a spitball at this girl in reading," Ozzie said. "But she ducked and it hit the teacher."

"They should make her come to the office for ducking," Christian said.

Mr. Davidson called them all into his office at the same time.

"Christian, you have detention for the next week," he said, without looking up. "Oswaldo, the same goes for you. Both of you can leave now, and make sure that you report to detention starting this afternoon at five past three."

"How long we have to stay?" Christian asked.

"Until you're told that you can leave," Mr. Davidson said.

"My mother wants to know where I am after school," Christian told him. "So I got to know or else I can't stay."

"You'll stay until three thirty," Mr. Davidson said. "Now the two of you are dismissed."

When Christian and Oswaldo had left, Mr. Davidson pointed to the wooden bench in his office. Jamal went and sat on it.

The bell rang and the morning announcements were made: "Everybody who didn't turn in their field-trip slips has to turn them in by this Wednesday. Anybody who wants to be in the chess club, please come down to room three-oh-eight at two o'clock. You have to have permission from your homeroom teacher. Also, the girl's volleyball team will have their first tryouts this afternoon in the gym. Wear your sneakers."

The class bell rang, and Jamal could hear shuffling through the hallways. Mr. Davidson went through some papers on his desk without looking at Jamal.

"Mr. Davidson." Miss Rose came in from the outer office. "Dwayne is here."

Dwayne came in with a tall, wide-shouldered woman. She wore glasses, but Jamal could see that she looked like Dwayne. The woman looked over at Jamal, letting her eyes rest on him as he looked back at her.

"Is this the one?" she said.

Dwayne nodded.

"Will you repeat your story, Dwayne?" Mr. Davidson closed the wide red pen he had and leaned back in his chair.

"He had a gun." Dwayne mumbled under his breath.

"I want to hear the whole story," Mr. Davidson said.

"I don't understand why you don't have the police here," the woman said.

"Mrs. Parsons." Mr. Davidson took his glasses off. "If the charges can be shown to be true, I will call the police. I can't call the police on the word of one child. It's as simple as that."

"He threatened my son with a gun and you say you can't call the police?" Mrs. Parsons stood up.

"Perhaps you can afford a lawsuit if you accuse this boy of doing something that he actually didn't to," Mr. Davidson said. "I can't risk putting the school in that position."

Mrs. Parsons sucked her teeth and looked away.

"Go on, Dwayne," Mr. Davidson said.

"He was messing with me in class and then we got into a fight in the storeroom." Dwayne's voice was just above a whisper. "Then he pulled out a gun."

"Jamal?"

"Everybody in the class—including Darnell, Tamia, Christian, and all of them—can tell you he

137

was the one messing with me. He said he was going to beat me up in the storeroom. First we had a fight outside, then the next day he said he was going to beat me up in the storeroom. You can ask anybody."

"What happened in the storeroom?"

"We had a fight."

"And was there a gun?" Mr. Davidson asked.

"There wasn't no gun," Jamal said. "He just got mad because I tore his shirt."

"Why would Dwayne say he had a gun if he didn't have one?" Mrs. Parsons said. Jamal could see she was mad.

"Why he want to fight me in the first place?" Jamal asked.

"I wasn't talking to you!" Mrs. Parsons raised her voice.

"It's the school's position not to make hasty accusations," Mr. Davidson said.

"It's the school's policy," Mrs. Parsons said, "not to make waves. I'm not sending my child to no school to be shot by this or any other hoodlum. I'm going to see a lawyer this afternoon."

"That's certainly your—"

Dwayne's mother was up and out the door, calling to Dwayne as she left. Dwayne stood, not looking over in the direction of Jamal before leaving.

"You bring your mother into school tomorrow morning," Mr. Davidson said to Jamal. "You're going to sit downstairs in the lunchroom every day until you do bring her to school, do you understand that?"

"She can't come," Jamal said. "She got to work."

"Then you'll just sit in the lunchroom," Mr. Davidson said. "I'm sure you won't miss a thing. Now you go to the lunchroom and report to Mr. Singh. I'm going to call him, and he'll be expecting you."

Mr. Singh was who they sent you to when you were in big trouble. Some of the older kids said that he beat kids, but Jamal didn't believe that. He did believe that he was big and mean. He had seen him make a kid cry once.

"Can I go down to the art room instead?"

"The art room? Don't you understand anything?"

"I didn't have no gun in school!"

"I sure hope not," Mr. Davidson said. "Not for your sake, because I don't think you're going to change. But I think too much of this school to let you spoil it for the rest of the children."

"What you want to see my mother for?"

"I hope that maybe, just maybe, I can convince her to take you out of this school," Mr. Davidson said. "Maybe put you someplace for kids with serious problems, or someplace that you're not going to contaminate everybody else. Now get down to the lunchroom right now!"

Jamal went down to the first floor, then into his homeroom. He went to the closet, got his coat, and left school.

●

"Jamal!" Sassy called to Jamal from her room.
"What?"

"A lady from your school called today and said you left in the middle of the day."

"She told that to Mama?"

"No, she told me."

"What did you say?"

"I said we knew, that Mama was home when you got home."

"What the lady say?"

"Something—I don't remember. How come you left school?"

"They messing with me."

"You going to tell Mama?"

"No, and don't you tell her. Okay?"

"Mama said when Tito came over Sunday he was crying."

"He okay."

"You and him going to run away?"

"No. Why don't you go to sleep."

●

Abuela was sick. Tito said that at first she just wouldn't talk to him, but then he could tell that she was sick.

"She didn't even ask about where the gun was," Tito said. They were walking along under the elevated trains along Broadway.

"Maybe she just still mad," Jamal said.

"No, she's sick," Tito said. "You come to the house."

It was nearly seven o'clock when they got to Tito's house. They went in and sat in the kitchen. Tito looked around and pointed toward Abuela's bedroom.

"Go in and see how she doing," Jamal said.

Tito looked at Jamal for a long minute, then got up and went into his grandmother's bedroom.

Jamal looked at the clock on the wall. There was a mass card taped to the wall above it.

Tito's house was different than his. Everything seemed older, but really nice. There was a cup filled with pencils on a dark wood cabinet. He had seen Tito's plates. The ones he ate on were white with small red stripes around them. But he had others, too, that he said Abuela had brought with her from Puerto Rico years before. They had a picture of a man and a woman who looked as if they came from George Washington's times, but they both had dark hair and the man carried a violin. There was a large platter on the wall with the same design.

Jamal saw a sheet of paper on the cabinet. He picked it up and saw that it was clean on both sides. He took a pencil from the cup and started drawing the design on the plate.

He had finished one of the figures, and it hadn't come out too badly, when Tito came out of the room. Abuela was with him.

"Hello." Jamal stood up.

"Hello, Jamal." Abuela's voice was weak. "How are you?"

"Fine."

"Did you have anything to eat?"

"I ate before," Jamal said. "How you feeling?"

"Not too good. But you know I'm not too young."

"I hope you feel better," Jamal said.

"You draw pictures?" Abuela took the picture that Jamal had drawn as she sat down.

"Yes, ma'am."

"Pictures! Little boys draw pictures. This is what I want Tito to do. Draw pictures like a little boy."

"Tito can't draw," Jamal said, smiling.

"It's okay." The old woman stood and started back toward the bedroom.

"Are you okay, Abuela?"

"Tired," she said. "So tired."

"You want anything, Abuela?" Tito asked.

The boys watched her as she went toward the door, stopped, and turned around. "Jamal, tell me that Tito is a good boy."

"Tito's always good," Jamal said. "He don't do nothing wrong. Really."

"That's good."

•

When Jamal got to the bodega, Indian and Angel were waiting for him. Indian was sitting on the counter, and Mr. Gonzalez was standing in the middle of the floor with a baseball bat.

"These your friends?" Mr. Gonzalez looked at Indian.

"What you doing here?" Jamal asked them.

"I'm calling you out," Indian said. "You want to

142

lead the Scorpions, then you got to be a leader. No jive leader, man. You got to get down. Can you get down?"

Jamal looked over at Mr. Gonzalez, who still held the bat in his hands.

"I don't want no trouble in the store," Jamal said.

"Yeah, uh-huh, you looking around to see what's shaking and everything, but I'm going to tell you what's shaking. The Indian is the chief, baby. That's my say, but I'm going to give you a play, 'cause that's my way, dig?"

"Go on."

"The man with the long bread needs some legs, dig? Now we got to rap about who running the show so the man don't get confused."

"I can't talk about it now," Jamal said.

"Yeah, well, you let me know when you can, and don't take forever doing it, 'cause I ain't got that much time."

Indian took a handful of candy bars from the counter. Jamal looked at him and saw that he looked high. He watched as Indian slid off the counter and walked slowly down the middle of the store. He stopped at the small card tables where the other dominoes players were still sitting and knocked over the dominoes.

Indian left the store first, brushing by a small boy who was coming in with a bottle under his arm. Angel stopped in the doorway and formed his hand into the shape of a pistol and shook it twice in Jamal's direction.

"Your brother's gone, man," he said. "You next."

•

Jamal didn't say anything when Mr. Gonzalez told him he had to leave. He didn't even blame him. Mr. Gonzalez started to pay him, and one of the dominoes players tried to stop him.

"Don't give him anything," the guy said. "You see what they took? They didn't pay one cent for what they took."

"I don't want to owe him anything," Mr. Gonzalez said.

He gave Jamal twenty-one dollars. "Look, let me tell you." The brown-skinned man's voice cracked as he spoke. "Those boys are going to jail. You stay away from them."

Jamal left the store. He had the twenty-one dollars in his hand when he left the store, and then pushed them into his pocket. It was the first time he had ever been paid for a job, and now the job was gone. Indian and Angel just came in and took his job. Threw it away. They were bigger than he was, and tougher. He knew it and they knew it. Everybody in the whole world knew it. Even the dominoes players in the store knew it. If Mr. Gonzalez hadn't wanted to give him the money, he wouldn't have had to. Jamal stopped at the corner and punched the wall with his fist until he couldn't stand it anymore.

CHAPTER FOURTEEN

As soon as he opened the door, Jamal knew something was wrong. The lights were out, and Sassy was sitting in the dark.

"Where's Mama?"

"She had to go to the hospital," Sassy said. "Randy got stabbed."

Jamal looked at Sassy, then went back to the door and made sure it was locked. What she had said didn't make any sense.

"How he get stabbed, when he in jail?" Jamal asked.

"He got stabbed in the jail."

"He okay now?"

"I don't know. Mama got a call from the jail, and she left right away. She left four dollars to get something to eat with. She said if she don't get back tonight and anything go wrong to call Mr. Stanton."

"She real upset?"

"Uh-huh."

"They think Randy gonna die?"

"I don't know. I spent part of the money."

"The four dollars?"

"Uh-huh. I bought some food for supper."

"How much money did Mama have?"

"I don't know. You want me to make supper? I can do it."

"Go ahead."

Sassy got up and turned the lights on and started to make supper. Jamal put the television on. He didn't want to think about Randy being stabbed. He didn't want to think about anything happening to the family. It seemed like they never made things happen to anybody else, or even for themselves. Things happened to his family, the same way things happened to him.

He was feeling small, the way he sometimes did. Small and weak. He tried to bring his mind to the television. The program was all about some white people who lived in the olden days. There were some kids on the program, and Jamal wondered if he could beat any of them. He couldn't fix it in his mind that he could. Anybody could say anything to him or do anything to him. He didn't even think it mattered that he wasn't a man yet. Most of the men he knew weren't doing that good either—they just talked tougher.

Jamal thought about Indian. Maybe he knew about Randy being stabbed. What had he said? *Your brother's gone, man. You next.* Then Angel had fixed his hand like he was shooting at Jamal. He didn't want to fight Indian. He couldn't win even if he did. He couldn't even beat Dwayne, and Dwayne was nothing but a kid next to Indian.

There wasn't much he could do. He couldn't take care of Mama, he didn't know what to do about Randy. Nothing. He couldn't even make Indian and Angel leave the bodega, and now he didn't even have a job. All his plans for saving money were gone too.

Sassy turned the fire under the chicken down low.

"You know, I saw Darnell the other day, and he asked me if you were the head of the Scorpions."

"I am."

"He said you had a gun in school too."

"I didn't have no gun in school."

"He said you had a fight with a kid and you had a gun."

"He so jive he don't know what he talking about."

"You going to get in trouble, just like Randy."

"Why, because Darnell lie all the time? Where you know him from?"

"If you brought your butt to church sometime you'd know Sister Jenkins is his grandmother."

"Sister Jenkins is Darnell's grandmother?"

"What I say?"

"I didn't know that."

"You got a gun?"

"I told you I didn't have no gun."

"Where it at?"

"Later for you!" Jamal got up, grabbed his jacket, and headed for the door.

"If it's in the house, I'm going to find it soon as you gone."

Jamal turned and looked at Sassy. He sat down on the couch. Sassy opened some of the packets of soy sauce they had got with take-out Chinese food, opened them, and poured the contents on the chicken.

"I'm thinking about throwing the gun away," Jamal said.

"That the same gun Randy shot that man with?"

"I don't know."

"You had it all the time?"

"I got it from Mack."

Sassy put on water for rice and started turning the chicken over. "Can I see the gun?"

"It's at Tito's house," Jamal said.

Sassy finished making supper. She had made rice, peas, and the fried chicken. The chicken was too salty, but it was okay. Then they watched television for a while, until Sassy fell alseep on the other end of the couch, away from Jamal.

Everything he could do came into Jamal's mind. He could sneak the gun out of the couch when Sassy went to bed and throw it away. He could take it somewhere and hide it. Maybe he could take it to Mack and tell him that he didn't want to be the head of the Scorpions. That's what he could do. He would hide the gun and then tell Mack that he didn't want to be part of the Scorpions anymore.

"Hey, Sassy!"

Sassy didn't move, and Jamal slid over to where she was curled against the armrest and shook her gently.

"Hey, Sassy!"

"What?" she murmured.

"Sassy, wake up!"

Sassy opened her eyes, wiped her mouth with the back of her hand, and said that she hadn't been sleeping.

"Look, do me a favor, okay?"

"What?" She took her legs from under her and put them down.

"Don't tell Mama about the gun. I'll take it out tonight and throw it away. Okay?"

"I thought you said it was at Tito's house."

"Just don't tell Mama, okay?"

"Why you bring it in here, anyway?"

"Are you gonna tell Mama?"

"I don't know."

"That's just like you," Jamal said. "You tell her everything and get her upset, and then she starts crying or feeling bad, and then you talking about how you sorry."

"You the one be doing stuff all the time."

"One thing I don't be doing is hurting Mama."

"I don't know," Sassy said. "Maybe I'll tell her and maybe I won't."

"You ain't nothing. You sure ain't family. 'Cause if you—"

"Don't jump up in my face 'cause you got a gun."

"Guns ain't half as bad as people like you."

"I didn't shoot at anybody."

"If it wasn't for people talking on Randy—big-mouth people like you—he wouldn't even be in jail today."

"You the one that said you didn't care about him being in jail!"

"Why don't you tell Mama I said it again so she can get more upset!"

Sassy started crying.

"You can tell her I made you cry, too," Jamal said. "Then maybe she get one of her headaches and you can get real happy about that, too!"

There was a stupid movie on about a woman trying to get on a man's basketball team, Jamal wanted to take the gun out and get rid of it before Mama got home, but more than that he wanted to make sure that Sassy didn't tell her.

"I'm gonna get rid of it," Jamal said.

Sassy didn't answer.

"The only reason I took it to school is because Dwayne was always picking on me," Jamal said. "He's bigger than me, a lot bigger."

"You shoot at him?"

"No. You gonna tell Mama?"

"Darnell said you telling people you the head of the Scorpions."

"He must think he the *Daily News* or something." Jamal took the cushion off the couch and reached down between the armrest and the side until he found the gun. "I'm going to get rid of it now. You can tell Mama anything you want to."

"Let's see it."

"No."

"If you don't let me see it I'm going to tell," Sassy said.

"So go on and tell," Jamal said. "Maybe I can go to jail too. Then you can have the whole house to yourself."

Jamal slipped on his coat and put the gun in the pocket just as he heard the key in the door. He looked over at Sassy, slipped the gun out of his pocket, and put it back in the couch. He put his coat back in the closet just as Mama came into the house.

"How Randy?" Jamal asked.

"They think he's going to live," Mama said.

"What happened?"

"They cut him up real bad," Mama said. Her hair wasn't combed, and Jamal could see a big patch where she didn't have much hair on one side. "He say he didn't know who did it. The man from the State said that's what they always say, because they know they got to go back in with the same ones that done it."

"You see Randy, Mama?" Sassy asked.

"I seen him. They got tubes going in him here and tubes going in him there, and he's all bandaged. . . ."

Mama opened her mouth, and a loud noise came out. It didn't sound like crying. It sounded more like something big that was wounded. Sassy jumped a little. Jamal got up and went to his mother. He put his arm around her. It wasn't like her to cry out loud like that. He remembered sometimes hearing her cry when she was in her bedroom alone, but not out loud like that.

Sassy turned the television off.

Mama took deep breaths and held on to the side of the chair she was sitting on.

"Mama, you all right?" Sassy asked.

"I'm all right," Mama said. "I know I got to get Randy out that jail before they kill him. I know I got to get him out."

There were footsteps in the hallway, and Jamal looked to see if the chain was on the door. It was.

The knock on the door was firm.

"I ask Reverend Biggs if he would come up and pray with us for Randy tonight," Mama said.

Sassy went to the door and asked who it was. Reverend Biggs's voice came through the tin-covered door, and Sassy opened it.

"How the boy, Sister Hicks?" Reverend Biggs was a tall, tan-skinned man with wide shoulders that hunched slightly forward as he walked. He wore thick glasses that made his eyes look small, and his hair was never really combed neatly. But the thing that Jamal liked about him was his voice. His voice was loud, deep, and warm, and seemed to fill the room as he spoke.

"He fighting for his life, Reverend Biggs," Mama

said. "I just hoped that maybe a word or two with God could help him."

"Well, I can understand that." Reverend Biggs took off his coat. "And if I can understand how you feel, you know the Lord does."

"Amen."

"Tell me what happened."

"They don't even know," Mama said. "They got to fighting up there and cut him up something terrible."

"The guards did that?"

"No, some of the other prisoners," Mama said.

"Lord have mercy!"

Jamal looked over at Sassy. She was sitting near the television, but her eyes were on Mama. Jamal knew that if Mama kept crying, Sassy would cry too.

"You know, Reverend Biggs, Randy never did walk a path like he was supposed to," Mama said. "And I know they convicted him of taking somebody's life, but that don't mean he ain't my flesh and blood."

"Sometimes the herbs we take are bitter, sister, but we got to take them anyway. The important thing here is that, as much as your heart is with your boy in the hospital, you got to hold your family here together too. We can't let the bad mess up the good."

"Amen." Mama was crying again.

"Sometimes when things get hard, we tend to set

our sights on what's hard, that difficult thing that keeps us upset, and we turn our backs on our strengths."

"I'm trying to keep these children on the right path," Mama said.

Jamal eased up off the cushion just enough to straighten it out a little. Through the doorway Jamal saw a roach crawl alongside a crack in the yellowed kitchen wall. It followed the crack halfway down the wall and then, as if it knew where it was going, veered off and took another route down behind the sink.

"We're going to say a few words for Randy, and ask God to look upon him kindly. Let's just everybody come into the kitchen and stand for a minute," Reverend Biggs said. "I don't think God needs us down on our knees. He don't care about our knees anyway—it's our hearts that He's looking at."

Jamal and Sassy went into the kitchen. Jamal stood near the refrigerator and Sassy near the stove.

"Bow your heads, children." Reverend Biggs was sitting at the table with Mama and put both of his hands on hers.

"Lord Jesus, we are gathered here at this midnight hour in sorrow and in pain. Our hearts are heavy, and the cup of our souls runneth over with grief.

"Tonight, Lord, we're praying for Sister Hicks's family. Not just her boy whose fate you hold cradled in the palm of Your great hand, but all her family.

We're asking You to spare all their lives and keep them all from harm, Lord.

"We're asking You to let your mercy rain down on this family so that their hearts will be filled with the peace that only You can give.

"Lord, lift the awful burden from this mother's heart. For when she lay down in a bed of pain to give birth to Randy, when she saw that she had brought another man-child into the world, she rose up from that bed with high hopes. Let her rise up with high hopes again, Lord Jesus. Let her look forward to the day that she can grow old and look upon her children with pride and love.

"Let her and her family find the way to turn to Thee in deed and prayer, and give them the strength to continue in thy grace from this moment on, as we join in Thy great prayer. . . .

"Our Father, who art in heaven, hallowed be Thy name. Thy kingdom come. Thy will be done, on earth as it is in heaven. Give us this day our daily bread, and forgive us . . ."

Jamal glanced over at Sassy. His sister had both of her eyes closed and her hands folded in front of her face. He knew Mama wouldn't let him go out tonight, so he would have to throw the gun away the next day.

". . . I really appreciate you coming out tonight, Reverend, and having this word of prayer and comfort for us," Mama was saying. "It just seems so hard sometimes."

155

"It's a hard life sometimes, Sister Hicks," Reverend Biggs said. "And the biggest temptation is to let how hard it is be an excuse to weaken."

"Well, we gonna be as strong as we can be," Mama said.

When Reverend Biggs left, Mama asked if they had eaten. Sassy said that they had. Jamal didn't say anything.

"Jamal, what's wrong with you, baby?"

"Ain't nothing wrong with me, Mama."

"I can't stand to have you weak, Jamal," Mama said. "I can't stand it now."

"I'm okay, Mama," Jamal said.

"How you doing, Sassy?"

"I'll be okay as long as you okay, Mama," Sassy said.

Jamal fell asleep almost as soon as he went to bed. When Sassy woke him up, he thought it was Mama at first.

"I didn't tell Mama about the gun," Sassy said.

"I thought you would be okay," Jamal said.

"Jamal, did you like Randy a lot?"

"Sometimes," Jamal said. "Sometimes."

"Sometimes I didn't like him that much," Sassy said. "Because he was always running around and things."

"Yeah, I know what you mean."

"I hope God don't let him die just because I didn't like him sometimes," Sassy said softly. "I like him okay now."

"God ain't gonna let him die, Sassy. Everything is gonna be okay."

Sassy kissed Jamal on his forehead and went back to bed.

Jamal lay in the darkness and thought about what Mama had said about him not being weak. The thing was that it was hard to be strong. It was really hard.

CHAPTER FIFTEEN

"So what you going to do?" Tito and Jamal stood on the corner of the school.

"I'm going to take the gun back over to Mack and tell him I don't want to be in the Scorpions no more," Jamal said.

"Why you going to do it now? Why don't you wait until after school?"

"I told you what Indian said in the store, man," Jamal said. "I think he looking for a way to chump me off so he can take over the Scorpions. If he try to mess with me, I'm gonna mess with him."

"I don't want you shooting nobody, Jamal."

"You coming with me?"

"How come you can't wait?" Tito's voice sounded whiny.

"'Cause I want to find Mack and give him the gun and tell him before I see Indian."

Tito looked toward the school. "Okay."

"You don't have to come if you don't want to," Jamal said.

"Why you always got to say that? Don't I always come with you?"

"Come on."

"You got the gun now?"

"Yeah."

The crack house was the only store on the whole block that never closed up. Jamal had heard that in the back, behind the ply board and the curtains, there was a room made of steel where the crack dealers put the crack in the little vials.

One of the guys sitting on folding chairs outside the house was eating scrambled eggs and potatoes from a silver tinfoil dish. He was dark, with a long head and an earring in his left ear. He stopped Jamal and Tito by putting his leg across the door.

"What y'all want?"

"We looking for Mack," Jamal said.

"Ain't no Mack around here" was the quick answer. The guy put a big forkful of eggs in his mouth.

"I'm going in to look around," Jamal said.

"Yo, man." The long-headed lookout pointed toward the avenue. "All you got to do is to relax your little narrow ass, and the wind will blow you down the street. If you keep your little narrow ass uptight, then I'll kick it down the street."

Jamal took the gun from his coat pocket and put in his belt.

"I don't like to be messed with, man," Jamal said.

"You threatenin' me?" The guy put his breakfast down on the ground next to him.

"You threatenin' me?"

"Who you?"

"We with the Scorpions," Jamal said.

"The Scorpions? I thought Mack wasn't with the Scorpions no more. That's what Indian said."

"That ain't what I said." Jamal straightened up and tried to look taller.

The guy looked at Jamal, then picked up his breakfast. He called into the darkness of the store.

"Yo, Tony! Come here a minute!"

"What's up?" Tony was blade thin, with red, slicked-back hair. He came to the door holding a two-way radio in his hand.

"They looking for Mack. You seen him?"

"Yeah, he in the park with all them other winos," Tony said.

"You got it, little brothers." The guy eating his breakfast leaned his chair back against the building.

The morning was just starting good. A few people were moving. Two women, one pregnant, were pushing a shopping cart full of clothes into the laundromat. Some kids, already late for school, were sauntering slowly down toward 120th Street.

A short black man who looked as if he were wearing makeup was opening the gates of the Audrey Woods funeral parlor.

But most of the people were just hanging out. Some teenagers were gathering on a stoop halfway down the block. The older men had already claimed the two corners on the avenue and were calling across the street to one another.

"I don't like this park, man," Tito spoke under his breath to Jamal.

"How come?"

"You got guys laying on the ground, you got guys laying on the grass, you even got some women laying around in here."

"They either winos or crackheads," Jamal said.

"They look like they thrown-away people," Tito said. "That makes me scared, because I don't want to be no thrown-away guy."

"That's why we got to be like this"—Jamal held up two fingers close together—"so we don't let nobody throw us away."

"There goes Mack." Tito nodded toward a bench where several men and two boys sat.

Jamal took a deep breath and went over to see him.

●

"We got to talk," Jamal said.

"Hey, I got to talk to you, too," Mack said.

He led them away from the bench he had been sitting on. His breath smelled of stale, sweet wine, and his eyes were bloodshot. "How Randy?"

Jamal looked at Tito, then back at Mack. "You know he got cut?"

"The word all over the street," Mack said. "A girl who live on Lenox Avenue was up there the other day, and she heard from her boyfriend that Randy got messed up."

"My moms is going to see him today," Jamal said.

"Indian trying to make his own deal now." Mack slowed down in front of a park bench. He put his hands on the bench and eased himself onto it.

"He dealing with them crack people, right?" Tito stood a few feet away from Jamal and Mack.

"Yeah, that's where the money is," Mack said. "Some guys from crosstown trying to push they stuff over here, and the Man want the Scorpions to light them up."

"He want us to kill them?" Jamal said.

"Yeah, but now Indian saying *he* the man and Angel his warlord," Mack said. "We can't be letting Indian just take over the Scorpions."

"They listening to Indian?" Jamal asked.

"Yeah, because they don't want nobody that can do no time working with them," Mack said. "I go down again, they got to get me as an adult. Everybody know that. They say Mack too old to be in the streets."

"I don't know," Jamal turned away. "Maybe we should just let Indian do his thing."

"Can't let that go down," Mack said. "No way. Indian get the big money, then he got everything. If you do the thing, then you get the money and we can get Randy out. If Indian do the thing, he gonna cop the money, then he gonna try to mess you up so they won't be no comeback."

"How much money they talking about?" Jamal asked him.

"Jamal, we don't want to kill nobody," Tito said.

"They talking about fi' thousand dollars," Mack said. "That ain't no chump change."

"I can't be killin' nobody," Jamal said, looking out over the park. "Maybe I ain't got the heart or something."

"I know the dudes they talking about," Mack said. "They some Spanish boys from over near Park Avenue. I can do the thing myself."

"Why don't you take over the Scorpions?" Jamal said. "I can get in touch with Randy and tell him you holding it together for him. Long as I'm only twelve, they gonna keep messing with me."

"They ain't gonna mess with you if they know you ain't scared to use the piece," Mack said. "Ain't nobody in no big hurry to kick out. You still got the piece, right?"

"Yeah." Jamal looked down the street at some kids playing Chinese handball against a building. "But I was thinking it might be cool if you was the head of the Scorpions. You Randy's ace and everything."

"No, man. They call a meeting and Indian be running his games 'cause he know my school thing ain't too tough. That's why me and Randy was tight. He had that reading and mess down pat and he didn't run no games. You know, he did his thing and I did mine and everything was everything. That's the way I figure it can be with me and you. That

163

way we can work a show and cop the bread for Randy's appeal."

"I got to think on it, man," Jamal said. "I'll see you around."

"Yeah, that's fresh," Mack said. "Look, can you help me out with ten dollars?"

Jamal looked at Tito, then reached into his pocket and pulled out the money he had got from Mr. Gonzalez. He gave Mack ten dollars, then started away.

"I thought you were going to give him the gun back," Tito said.

"You see all them people in the park?"

"I got a bad feeling," Tito said.

"I'm supposed to take out the gun in front of everybody?"

"You took it out in front of the crack house," Tito said. "I think you like that gun, man."

"I just got to think about what Mack was saying," Jamal said. "Ain't nothing wrong with thinking before you do something."

"Mack's bad news too," Tito said. "I think he using that crack."

"You think I can't tell that?"

"So?"

"So come with me when I talk to Indian?"

"What you going to say?"

"Maybe I'll say he should give me the money to get Randy out and then I won't be the head of the Scorpions no more."

"Maybe you should tell him that's what Randy said."

Jamal stopped and looked at Tito. "Hey, that's real cool. I'll tell him that Randy said that Mack can still be the warlord if he want, but he don't have to be."

"You think Mack is going to bother you?"

"No, I think he into that wine and crack. He'll be all messed up soon," Jamal said. "That's your best idea all year."

"Hey, they don't call me Tito the Kid for nothing," Tito said. "When you going to see Indian?"

"You want to go now?"

"Suppose Mack come over?"

"He getting his head bad," Jamal said. "You see how his nose was running and what he want to borrow?"

"Ten dollars for the crack," Tito said.

When they got over to the firehouse, only Blood was there. Jamal told Blood he had something important to tell Indian and had to see him right away. Blood said he didn't know where Indian was.

"You can go over to Griff's in about a hour," Blood said. "Sometime he drop by there."

"Yeah," Jamal said. "You see him, tell him I want to talk to him."

"Yeah."

Tito and Jamal walked slowly up to Griff's Bar-B-Que Joint. They stopped across the street to see if they could see who was inside. The windows were steamed, and they couldn't tell.

"Gimme your pencil," Jamal said.

Tito gave him his pencil, and Jamal wrote down the telephone number next to the We Deliver sign.

•

Jamal still had some money from Mr. Gonzalez. He and Tito went over to Broadway and stopped for pizza and sodas, and then they stopped in a candy store and Jamal bought two boxes of Good and Plenty and a drawing tablet.

"This is an official drawing tablet," Jamal said. "You can't write letters or anything on it because it wouldn't even fit in an envelope. All you can do with it is draw on it."

"What you going to draw?"

"Maybe I'll draw you," Jamal said. "And if it comes out real good, I'll give it to Abuela."

"Or you can give it to Sassy."

"Sassy? I wouldn't even give her a picture."

"How come?"

"You got to give pictures to people who like pictures and stuff," Jamal said. "You take my father. He don't like pictures. I think he don't like pictures. Maybe he just don't like me."

"I think he likes you."

"Sit over here and I'll start drawing you," Jamal said. They were at Grant's Tomb. It was the only official place that kids could hang out in. Jamal liked how big and solid the place looked, and how quiet it was. He could sit on the low wall around the tomb and look down into Harlem, or he could look the other way into Riverside Park. Sometimes he would look down at where the tombs that held Grant and his wife were, but mostly he didn't.

"You better make me look good," Tito said.

"You don't look too good to start with." Jamal smiled.

"Yeah, but you can make me real handsome, right?"

"You think your father like you?" Jamal asked. "I mean, I know he *likes* you, but you think he likes you a lot?"

"I don't know," Tito said. "He said he'd be glad when I wasn't around Abuela so much. I don't know why he said that, because he's the one that moved back to Puerto Rico and let me stay here."

"Open your coat up a little."

"No, it's too cold."

"It ain't cold," Jamal said. "And suppose you were a girl. You might have to pose naked."

"I wouldn't pose naked."

Jamal worked on the drawing for almost half an hour. An old woman came by and looked at it, and then a man and a woman. They watched Jamal draw for a while, said that they liked the drawing, and went on. As soon as they left, Jamal started laughing.

"You making a messed-up drawing?" Tito asked.

"No, it's real nice."

167

"Then why you laughing?"

"Because it makes me feel funny to have people come and watch me draw," Jamal said. "When you go down to the Village, that's what people be doing. Standing around and watching the artists draw. That's really fresh."

"Suppose Indian say okay, he's going to be the leader of the Scorpions," Tito said. "You going to throw the gun away?"

"Maybe I'll hide it someplace," Jamal said.

"If you don't throw it away, then you still got it," Tito said.

"I was just thinking that if I—hold your head still—"

"My nose itches—"

"Scratch it real quick," Jamal said. "I was just thinking that if somebody starts messing with me, I could make them stop if I had the gun. I don't mean just anybody—I mean somebody big. Or if somebody mess with Mama."

"You remember that time I got into a fight with that guy who had that white dog?"

"You didn't get into a fight with him. He just beat you up," Jamal said.

"Yeah, okay. But when that happened, I prayed real hard to God to make him die or something. Then he beat me up again, and I felt real bad again, but he didn't die and I didn't die so everything was okay. If I had a gun, maybe I would have shot him or something."

"If he knew you had a gun, he wouldn't mess with you. Suppose he started messing with you this afternoon. And all you had to do was take the gun around and show it to him and tell him that if he mess with you again you was going to shoot him, even if you wasn't really going to shoot him. If he started messing with you again, would you do it?"

"You mean scare him with the gun?"

"Yeah."

"Yeah," Tito said. "But only a big guy like that."

"That's what I'm talking about," Jamal said.

"I still got a bad feeling about it," Tito said. "I think that's because I'm a little scared of it."

"You a little scared of everything."

"Just a little," Tito said softly.

"Ain't nothing wrong with that," Jamal said. "Everybody's scared of something unless they using crack or something."

Jamal finished the drawing and signed it. Then he closed the pad.

"Let's see it," Tito said.

"You want to buy it?"

"Let's see it first."

"No, you got to buy it if you want to see it," Jamal said.

"That's 'cause you messed it up."

"Is that messed up?" Jamal asked, opening the tablet.

They both looked at the drawing. It did look like him. Tito gave Jamal the thumbs-up sign.

CHAPTER SIXTEEN

Jamal was going to tell Mama that he only had half a day of school, but nobody was home. Mama had gone back up to the hospital to see Randy, and Sassy was in school. He had checked the mailbox and had found the letter from Mr. Davidson. It couldn't be anything but trouble, he thought. At first he didn't open it, just put it in the bill can on top of the refrigerator. Then he thought it might be about the gun and opened it. It said that Mama had to call him at once. It didn't say anything about the gun. Dwayne's mother was right. The school didn't want any trouble about the gun.

"What you going to do?" Tito asked.

"I'll call him," Jamal said.

"You going to make believe you're your mother?" Tito's eyes widened.

"No, I'm just gonna tell him that she can't call him on account of Randy."

Jamal dialed the school number and waited for an answer. Finally the operator came on, and he asked for Mr. Davidson. He got Mrs. O'Connell.

"Hello, Mrs. O'Connell?"

"Who is this?" Mrs. O'Connell's voice sounded stern over the phone.

"This Jamal Hicks. My mother had to go up to Stormville because my brother, Randy, got stabbed, so she can't call Mr. Davidson until he get better."

"Hicks?"

"Jamal Hicks."

"One minute."

Music started coming over the phone as Mrs. O'Connell put Jamal on hold. Jamal put the phone up to Tito's ear.

"That's the same kind of music they got in elevators," Tito said.

"Jamal, why weren't you in school today?" Mrs. O'Connell's voice.

"Mr. Davidson said I can't go to classes until my mother comes to school."

"Where is your mother now?"

"She went up to the hospital."

"Where's the hospital?"

"I think it's right near the prison," Jamal said.

Jamal heard Mrs. O'Connell repeat to somebody what he had said. He could hear a man's voice say something, and then Mrs. O'Connell got back on the phone.

"Where was your brother when he was hurt?"

"He was in the jail they got up there."

Mrs. O'Connell repeated what Jamal had said, then got a reply.

"Okay, Jamal, you come in to school tomorrow. Report to Mr. Davidson's office as soon as you do."

"Yes, ma'am." Jamal hung up the phone.

"What she say?"

"I got to go to school tomorrow," Jamal said. "She said I got to go to Mr. Davidson's office in the morning. Probably got to hear him run his mouth again."

"You going to call Indian now?"

Jamal looked through his pockets until he found the number of Griff's Bar-B-Que Joint. He dialed it, and jumped when the phone was answered almost at once.

"Indian there?"

The voice on the other end of the phone was gravelly as he called Indian's name out loud. There was music in the background, but it wasn't the kind you heard in elevators.

"Who calling?" the gravelly voice barked into the phone.

"Jamal. Randy's brother."

Jamal waited a few minutes for someone to get on the line. He felt his stomach tighten up. He looked over at Tito, who was watching cartoons on television with the sound turned low.

"What you want?" A voice came on the line.

"This Indian?"

"No, this is Angel. What you want?"

Jamal took a deep breath and told Angel about Randy telling his mother that Indian should be the head of the Scorpions. He looked over at Tito, who was now watching him. Tito tried to smile, but he was too nervous.

"He said the Scorpions should get the money together for his appeal," Jamal said.

Angel got off the phone, then the gravelly voice came back on and said that Jamal should call back because he had to use the phone.

"When should I call back?" Jamal asked.

"Don't make no difference to me." The answer was followed by a click as the phone went dead.

"What he say?"

"This other guy said I got to call back," Jamal said. "I just talked to Angel, anyway."

Tito turned up the cartoons again. "You going to feel good when you're not in the Scorpions anymore," he said.

"I'll be glad when things get back to normal," Jamal said.

"You know what we should do? Anybody fight us, we should fight them together," Tito said. "We don't even say anything, right? Somebody hit you, then we just walk up to him and both of us start fighting right away."

"That's a good idea. We get us a baseball bat too."

"You know what this guy I know got?" Tito started relacing his sneakers. "He got a blackjack made out of wire."

"That wire like on lamps and stuff?"

"Yeah."

173

"You fold it over like three times, and then you wrap the wire around it, right?"

"He folded it over about five times," Tito said. "He let me hit a garbage can with it. You should have heard how much noise that thing made."

Jamal called the barbecue joint again. When he asked for Indian, the gravelly-voiced guy cursed before he called him. Jamal heard him say not to be on his phone all day.

"Yo, man, this is Angel. Indian say you got to lay it down in front of the Scorpions so everybody know it's the real deal. You know where the swings and stuff is in the park?"

"What park?"

"Marcus Garvey."

"Yeah."

"He say he busy today, but you meet him there tomorrow night at eleven o'clock and say what you said about him being the head of the Scorpions."

"Why I got to meet him there?" Jamal asked.

"To show you ain't jive," Angel said. "If you don't show, it mean you trying to pull something, so you better be there."

Jamal told Tito what Angel had said. Tito bit his lip and looked back toward the television.

Neither one said anything while they watched an episode of *ThunderCats* that they both had seen before.

They watched television until half past three, when Sassy came home.

"Y'all go to school today?" Sassy asked when she saw Jamal and Tito draped over the chairs.

"We only had half a day," Jamal said.

"Is that right, Tito?" Sassy stood right in front of Tito so he couldn't look at Jamal.

"That's right," Tito said.

"You lying," Sassy said. "I can tell when you lying because you can't look me in the eye and say it."

"I can look you right in your eye and say it," Jamal said.

"Yeah, that's because you lie all the time," Sassy said. "Tito ain't used to lying."

"I can look you in the eye," Tito said.

"Look me in the eye." Sassy leaned close to Tito's face.

"I think she wants to kiss you, Tito."

"Jamal, why you so fresh?"

"You want me to be stale?"

"You are stale," Sassy said. "You just too dumb to know it."

"I ain't as dumb as you."

"Look me in the eye," Sassy said, getting in front of Tito again. "Now tell me that you had half a day."

"I had half a day today."

Sassy looked closely at Tito's eyes and said that maybe he was telling the truth.

Jamal walked Tito home.

"You know what Sassy didn't know?" Tito said.

"The whole time she was looking in my eyes, I had my fingers crossed."

"She can't tell if people lying anyway."

"Why you think Indian want to meet you tomorrow in the park?" Tito asked.

"So he can act like he a big man or something," Jamal said.

"Suppose he start something with you?"

"Remember what you said about being beaten up and then it's over and not too bad?"

"Yeah?"

"So that's what I'm going to do," Jamal said. "If he starts to beat me up, I'm just going to take it like a man. Then I'm going to walk away, and when I get home I'll just wash up and laugh at him."

•

The school nurse wasn't really funny, but everybody laughed at her anyway. She was real thin, and always smiled no matter what happened. If a kid got a cut on his hand, she would smile when she put a bandage on it. If you had an upset stomach, she would smile and give you something, then make you lie down on the couch. There were two things that Mrs. Roberts always did—make you lie down on the couch and give you a peppermint wrapped in cellophane. It was like a reward for being sick.

Jamal had never heard of anyone having to sit in the nurse's office when they got in trouble, but when Mr. Davidson took him there, that's what he thought he would have to do.

"Jamal, what we want you to do is to take this form home to your mother to sign. Does your mother read?"

"Yeah, she read," Jamal said. "You read?"

"I just asked," Mrs. Roberts said. "Have her read this form. Now, if there's anything she doesn't understand about it, she can always come in and discuss it with me."

"What's it for?" Jamal asked, looking at the form.

"It's for something we think will help you a lot," Mrs. Roberts said. "If you were just a little calmer in school, especially in the mornings, things would be a lot easier for all of us. Wouldn't you like that?"

"I guess so," Jamal said.

"Well, what we would like to do is to help you to stay calm by giving you a little bit of medicine and one of my famous peppermint candies."

"If she sign this, then she don't have to come to school?" Jamal asked.

"She should come and discuss your progress," Mr. Davidson said. "But we can try this first and see if it helps."

"Then she don't have to come to school?"

"Not for the time being," Mr. Davidson said.

"I'll give it to her," Jamal said.

●

"So what you guys going to do?" Darnell was standing between Dwayne and Jamal in the yard.

"It's up to him," Jamal said. "But I don't want to hear his mouth no more."

177

"My mother said if he mess with me anymore, she's going to sue the Board of Education."

"In other words"—Darnell took his cap off the back of his head and placed it over his heart—"you punking out!"

"My mother told me to stay away from him," Dwayne said.

"But if it wasn't for your mother, what would you do?"

Jamal looked at Dwayne and Dwayne looked away.

"He ain't got his gun with him, Dwayne." Tamia Davis pushed Dwayne toward Jamal. "Do something."

"Why don't you just shake hands and forget it?" Christian said.

"Why don't you just shut up?" Darnell said.

"Why don't you just *shut* me up, faggot!" said Dwayne.

Darnell looked Dwayne up and down, but he didn't try anything against the bigger boy.

Jamal wanted to shake hands and get it over with with Dwayne, but he knew if he went to shake first everybody would think that he was scared of Dwayne without his gun.

"What you want to do?" Dwayne looked at Jamal.

"You better do what your mama say," Jamal said. "Stay away from me."

He turned and walked away across the school yard.

Mama was talking really loud, the way she did sometimes when she was trying to get her nerve up. Sassy was talking loud too. She didn't have to get her nerve up; she was going along with Mama.

"I been working for that man for almost ten years," Mama was saying. "And he got more money than anybody in the world!"

"He know you going to pay it back," Sassy said.

"He don't even have to think about that," Mama said. "I don't owe nobody this side of the grave a dime that I don't pay back."

"A thousand dollars is a lot of money, but he got it," Sassy said.

"A thousand dollars ain't nothing to people with his kind of money," Mama said. "You know, they can go over to Atlantic City and lose that much money in a single day and not even worry about it."

"What he say when you asked him?"

"I told him not to say nothing," Mama said. "I want him to think on it for a while. When the lawyer said he thought that he could get Randy a new trial for a thousand dollars, I did some heavy thinking about it and some heavy praying on it."

"How come it only cost a thousand dollars now?" Jamal asked.

"'Cause they don't want to have to take care of him sitting up in the hospital," Mama said. "The lawyer say if he hurt in there, then they get anxious to get him out so they don't have to take care of him. They can let him on out and let the welfare take care of him. That way he don't be no trouble to them."

"Ain't nobody want no trouble," Jamal said.

"I don't see why he ain't called back," Mama said. "Maybe he looking for a way to explain it to Mrs. Stanton."

"What she like?" Sassy asked.

"I think she a little prejudiced," Mama said. "I only met her once or twice, but she acted real hincty."

"If he get the money, then how long before Randy get out?" Jamal asked.

"You know you got to go through the whole process." Mama had cut all the meat off the Kentucky Fried Chicken and had placed it in a pot of chicken broth along with some chopped broccoli. "He said it still might take two years, but just knowing that he getting out, that somebody working on his case, will keep his spirit up. You know you can die in them jails from just having a broken spirit."

"What he gonna do when he get out?"

"Go back to school," Mama said. "I'm seeing to that. Get something in his head so he can earn him a good living."

•

Jamal thought that if he worked the whole time, he could get the thousand dollars faster than two years. Maybe he would pay Mr. Stanton if he loaned

Mama the money. That way, when Randy got out, they wouldn't owe anything.

Mrs. Padgett called and said she had heard about Randy being stabbed, and said how sorry she was.

Jamal wanted to wait until after they had eaten to give Mama the note from school. Sometimes she signed things and didn't even act as if she was interested. Then sometimes she read things carefully.

The phone rang and Sassy got it. It was Mr. Stanton.

There wasn't any need for Jamal to ask what was being said on the telephone. It was all over Mama's face, in the sadness of her eyes and in the way her shoulders drooped before she sat down. When, after a long time, a time of telling Mr. Stanton how she understood how money was hard to come by and how she knew he wasn't having such a good year, she hung the phone up, she was crying.

"Lord, when am I going to learn that my problems don't belong to nobody but me?" Mama started rocking back and forth. "Lord, when am I going to *learn*?"

"I'll help get the money, Mama," Jamal said.

Mama looked at Jamal and beckoned him over to her. When he got to her, she put her arms around him and hugged him tightly. Then she saw Sassy and beckoned her over, and the three of them held each other and rocked quietly in the small room.

CHAPTER SEVENTEEN

From where he sat on Tito's stoop, Jamal could see the neon lights from the corner bar blink on and off. Nearer to him a gentle wind lifted a paper bag and made it dance along the street. Jamal watched as a cat came from beneath a car, arched its back, and hissed at the bag.

Two girls came out of the building. One of them smiled at Jamal as they passed. The aroma of their perfume lingered in the air behind them.

Abuela usually went to bed at nine, and Tito was supposed to come downstairs at nine thirty, but it was almost ten and he hadn't shown up. Jamal thought that maybe Abuela had caught him sneaking out. He wanted to go upstairs and knock on the door, but he didn't. Tito would show if he could, Jamal thought. That was the way Tito was.

"Hey, young blood, what you doing?" A rail-thin wino, his legs wide apart, stopped in front of Jamal.

"Get out my face," Jamal said.

"What? I ain't good enough for you, right?"

Jamal turned away. He was still thinking about Indian. Indian could beat him, he knew. But if just Indian was there, then he could take it. But if Angel was there too, then there would be a problem.

"You want me to tell you my story?" The wino shifted his position.

"No."

"That's 'cause you stupid," the wino said. "If you knew anything, then you would want to hear my story, see? Because I'm the same as you is."

"Get out my face, man," Jamal said. He had the gun in a paper bag on his lap.

"No, man, I used to be just like you," the wino said. "You couldn't tell me nothing. You know what I used to do?"

"Yeah, get drunk."

"That supposed to be smart, right?"

"Why don't you split?" Jamal said.

"I used to be a ball player. I could really hoop. No lie. I used to shake and bake."

"Yeah."

"Hey, I'm trying to tell you something. I'm trying to give you what you ain't got. You know what that is? Some smarts!"

The front door of Tito's building opened, and a stocky man filled it. He put his thumbs in his belt and looked from side to side. Then he hunched his shoulders twice and came down the stairs. Jamal watched him swagger down the street.

"He ain't nothing," the wino said. "He walk like he mean, but he ain't got the green! You know what I mean by the green?"

Jamal looked away. He didn't want to see the

wino. He didn't want to be like him, or look like him, or see him.

"Jamal!"

Jamal turned to see Tito, carrying a bag of garbage.

"How come you took so long?"

"I got the time all wrong," Tito said. "She goes into her bedroom at nine, but she don't go to sleep or something. I told her I was going to take the garbage out."

"Come on."

"I think I got to go back upstairs so she don't think I'm out," Tito said. "I'll go upstairs, and soon as she goes back in her room I'll sneak out."

"We supposed to be over to the park at eleven," Jamal said.

"I'll be right back," Tito said.

Tito put the garbage on the curb and went back into the building.

"That your boy?" the wino asked.

"Why?"

"You know he a Puerto Rican, don't you?"

"Yeah, I know."

"All them Puerto Ricans do is drink that tequila and get crazy," the wino said. "That's what makes them so old-looking. You see baby Puerto Ricans and old Puerto Ricans, that's all you see. You don't see no regular Puerto Ricans. You ever notice that?"

The red-and-yellow clock in the bar across the street from Tito's house showed that it was five minutes to eleven. They were going to be late. Jamal wanted to get it over with. He remembered what Angel had said about him not showing up.

"And if you get into a fight with a Puerto Rican, you got to look out in case he got a knife," the wino went on.

Jamal wondered if there would ever be a time in his life when he didn't have to worry about somebody beating him up, or being in a fight with somebody.

"Let's go!" Tito was in the doorway.

"Where's your coat?"

"I got two shirts on," Tito said.

"Remember what I told you about them Puerto Ricans!" the wino called after them.

"What happened?" Jamal asked.

"Abuela felt something was happening," Tito said. "She can feel things the same way you can see them. She kept her door open, and she sat right in front of it."

"How you get out?"

"I told her I heard something in the hallway," Tito said. "She gave me a look with her quiet eyes, but she didn't say nothing."

"What you mean?" They were already crossing in front of St. Joseph's. Jamal turned down and headed for 124th Street.

"How come you going down one twenty-fourth?"

"That's what I want to do," Jamal said. "I don't want Indian to know where I'm coming from. What you mean, she looked at you with her quiet eyes?"

"Sometimes," Tito said, hurrying to keep up, "she got regular eyes like regular people. Then sometimes she got quiet eyes. They get real calm, like she's tired or something, only you know she's not tired."

Jamal pictured Abuela's quiet eyes in his mind. He thought about drawing a picture of her. The picture would be light, but the eyes would be dark, almost like Tito's, and big, with the eyelids half closed. He knew what Tito meant about quiet eyes. Sometimes Mama had them too.

They didn't slow down until they reached Lenox Avenue. Jamal looked through the window at Thompson's barber shop. It was almost twenty past eleven.

"You going to give him the gun?" Tito asked. He had seen the bag that Jamal was carrying.

"First I got to see how he acting," Jamal said. "You hold the gun. Then if he act like everything is all right, I'll call you over and you give him the gun."

"Suppose he don't act like everything's okay?"

"If he hit me that's okay," Jamal said. "I'm just going to punk out and take it."

"You're not a punk."

"If that makes it okay with him, then I got to go along with it," Jamal said. "Only thing I'm worried about is if Angel is there. If he's there, then he might try to beat me up real bad. If that happen, then you start yelling and maybe they'll run or something."

"Suppose they don't."

"Then I'm gonna run," Jamal said.

"You scared?"

"No, man. I feel real calm, 'cause soon everything is going to be straight."

"If they try to beat you up real bad, maybe I can help," Tito said.

"All you gonna do is get beat up too."

"That's okay."

"If you were my brother, we'd be so tight," Jamal said. "We'd be like this." He crossed his fingers.

"We still like that," Tito said.

"We get big, we got to get us a boat," Jamal said. "Then we can ride it around and talk about how we used to be poor."

Jamal gave Tito the bag with the gun in it and started walking toward Marcus Garvey Park.

"Hey, Jamal?"

"What?"

"We going to let girls come on to our boat?"

"Only movie stars," Jamal said.

"Good."

●

There were some women hanging around the outside of the park, and Jamal thought they were probably hustlers, but when he got closer to them he saw that they were Jehovah's Witnesses.

"How would you like a free copy of a really good message?" one pretty Witness asked him.

187

Jamal shrugged her off and went on into the park. He turned back and saw the young woman still smiling at him.

Two policemen stood across the street in front of a social club. Both of them looked young. One of them was Spanish, and the other was white, with long hair.

Jamal and Tito looked at them awhile and then went into the park.

"You stay back so they don't see you," Jamal said. "If I start running or anything, you start running too. Okay?"

"Suppose they try to beat you up?"

"I'll take it," Jamal said. "Or I'll run or something. It's gonna be cool. You okay?"

Tito nodded.

Jamal pulled his coat closed in front and started toward the playground part of the park. He was scared, but he wasn't sure what he was scared of. He just wished that it was over.

The playground was full of shadows that danced along the wire fence and through the small circles of light made by the lights on top of the fence. Jamal stood still, trying to peer through the darkness, trying to ignore the shadows of the trees that moved before him. In the center of the playground there were swings. Only one of them was moving. It squeaked as Indian swung slowly back and forth.

Angel was leaning against one of the poles that held the swings up. The light in the playground was near the monkey bars, but Jamal could see Indian clearly.

Jamal took a deep breath and walked up to the fence that was around the swings.

"Yo, what's happening?" Jamal called out.

"You what's happening," Indian said.

"I thought you said you wanted some Scorpions here to hear what I had to say."

"I'm here." Indian pushed his feet against the ground and swung slowly. Two pigeons walked along the far side of the fence, pecking at a cellophane bag.

"Well, Randy told my mother he didn't want me to be the head of the Scorpions no more," Jamal said.

"Yeah, that's because he all cut up," Indian said. "I heard about it. He must have tried his big-time act in the slam, and they didn't go for it."

"He doing okay," Jamal said. "Anyway, he said that the Scorpions should get the money up for his appeal, and then you should be the leader."

"That's all you got to say?" Angel spoke from the shadows. "All you got to say is what Randy said?"

"I ain't got all night," Jamal said.

"You want some smoke?" Indian held out a joint.

"Unh-uh."

"Randy don't let him smoke yet," Angel said. When Randy say he can smoke, then he gonna get him some of them bubble-gum cigarettes."

"How come you didn't bring Mack with you?"

The swing had slowed down, and Indian was swinging slowly in the slight breeze. His eyes closed for a minute, then opened slowly. He was high. "Ain't Mack your warlord?"

"I don't need no warlord if I ain't gonna be in the Scorpions no more," Jamal said.

"Hold time—" Indian took a deep drag on his joint. "First you say you ain't the leader of the Scorpions, now you say you giving up the colors."

"That's the way it is," Jamal said.

"You don't give up the colors unless the leader say you can give them up," Angel said.

"I'm giving them up so there won't be no trouble," Jamal said. "I told Randy I was giving them up."

"Randy ain't the leader of the Scorpions," Indian said. "I'm the leader. You got to ask me."

Jamal looked up. The sky was clear, and way above the television antennas and rooftops a sprinkle of stars filled the night sky. It was funny, but he hardly ever looked at the stars at night. He was always looking straight ahead, or around him.

"Well, I'm giving up the Scorpions' colors," Jamal said.

"He telling you." Angel had edged closer. "He ain't asking, he telling you."

"Why you ain't so bad now?" Indian asked. "You ain't got your piece with you, huh?"

"He ain't got his wino Mack with him either," Angel said.

"If he was here, you wouldn't be talking so big," Jamal said.

"Yeah, but he ain't here," Indian said. "And I ain't scared of him anyway. But what it is—what it really is—is now you ain't got nothing to back you up 'cept what you got in your heart, sucker."

Jamal swallowed hard and took a step backward.

"I think me and you should get down to see who the leader of the Scorpions," Indian said. He took a deep drag on the joint, and Jamal heard it crackle. "What you think?"

Angel moved next to Jamal. He could smell his breath. He had been smoking reefer, maybe crack. Jamal took his hands off the fence. He looked over toward Indian, started to say that he didn't want to fight him, but nothing came out.

"I think he scared," Angel said.

Indian swung forward and came out of the swing. He was on the other side of the low fence from Jamal. Angel was on the same side Jamal was on.

"You scared, punk?" Indian moved his face toward Jamal's, but his eyes looked as if they were looking at something far away.

Jamal stepped back from the fence, and Angel got behind him and pushed him hard into it. Indian punched at his face and missed, and Jamal tried to turn away. Angel kicked him on the side of his leg. Jamal tried to spin away, but Indian caught him by the neck, pulling him backward and part of the way over the fence.

"Why you ain't so bad now?" Indian said. "How come you don't just get into your thing so that everybody know how bad you are?"

"We got to teach this sucker a lesson," Angel said. "Something that Randy going to hear about."

Jamal twisted away from Indian, but Angel punched him in the stomach. He doubled over, and Angel straightened him up so that Indian could grab him again.

"Tomorrow we got something for Mack," Indian said. "But tonight your turn."

Indian pulled Jamal back over the fence until his feet weren't touching the ground. Jamal grabbed at Indian's arm with both his hands, trying to twist out of his grip, trying to breathe.

He didn't see the punch coming, but he felt it as Angel hit him again. He felt his stomach turn, and he started to throw up.

Whoomph! Whoomph!

The blows came one after the other. Jamal thought he would pass out. He went down and found himself in a sitting position, the ground spinning around him. He saw Indian stumbling back toward the swing.

Jamal got to his hands and knees, his head spinning. The dim light faded in and out. Jamal felt Angel's knee against his shoulder, looked up, and saw Angel reaching into his pocket. He tried to crawl forward, but Angel's leg pinned him against the fence. He looked up as he heard the click and saw the flash of steel.

Crack! Crack!

There was a long pause.

Crack!

Jamal closed his eyes tightly and pulled his hand over his head.

He felt something fall against him, and then away.

"Jamal!"

He looked up. It was Tito.

"Get up!"

Jamal grabbed the fence and pulled himself up. He looked down and saw Angel lying on the ground. On the other side of the fence, Indian was crawling away.

"Come on!"

Jamal sucked in deep breaths of air and started after Tito. They ran into the darkness of the park, toward the east side. Jamal looked back. Nobody was following them. Outside the park a group of teenagers were dancing to the hard rhythms of a boom box.

CHAPTER EIGHTEEN

They ran out of the far end of the park, past the darkened tenements, until they couldn't run anymore. Jamal's lungs were burning and his legs ached. He leaned against a wall, head on his arm. Tito was ahead of him, almost flat against the brick wall, half hidden in the shadows.

Jamal went over to Tito without straightening up.

"You saved me, Tito." The words came in great rushes of breath. "You saved me. He was gonna stab me."

Tito's whole body shook with his sobs. Jamal put his arm around Tito and put his head on his shoulder while he tried to get his breath. He looked down the street. No one was following them.

"Where the gun?"

Tito looked down and seemed surprised to find that he still had the weapon in his hand. Jamal took it away from him.

"I'm throwing it away now, okay?"

Tito's face was puffed, and mucous mixed with the tears that ran freely. He nodded his head, and Jamal looked for a place to get rid of the gun.

There was a dumpster near the corner. There were boards sticking out from it. Jamal went over to it. It was higher than he was, but he could reach over the side. He looked around one more time and dropped the gun over the side. It didn't make any noise when it landed, and Jamal thought it must have landed on some garbage. He looked around, saw a trash can, and dumped it over the side of the dumpster too. He hoped the garbage would cover the gun. Then he went back to Tito, put his arm around him, and started back across town by way of 118th Street.

"He had a knife," Jamal said. "Did you see the knife?"

Tito nodded.

"I tried to just take it," Jamal said. "I was going to just take. I didn't even care how bad it was, but he was going to stab me."

Tito nodded. Then he stopped, put his hands on his knees, and threw up.

"If you children didn't drink that wine and use that dope, you wouldn't be getting sick in the street!" The woman's voice was as deep as a man's.

Jamal looked at her and then put his arm around Tito's shoulders. He thought about the playground, about what it might look like now. He imagined Angel lying near the fence, and maybe Indian on the other side of it. They didn't have to be hurt bad, he knew. Maybe they would be in the park now. Then, later, when they were all better, they would get the Scorpions to come after Jamal and Tito.

"Jamal." Tito's voice was soft and low.

"Tito, you okay?"

"I'm sorry."

"You saved my life."

"I didn't want to shoot nobody."

"I know, man." Jamal was holding one of Tito's arms. He felt it twitch under his grip. "You didn't want to do nothing like that, but Angel was gonna stab me."

Tito wasn't walking right. He staggered, and Jamal thought he was going to fall. They stopped near a bar, and Jamal looked at Tito in the blue light from the neon piano in the bar's window.

"You okay, Tito?"

He didn't look okay. He looked as if somebody had drawn his face and just made dark holes where the eyes should have been.

Tito was shaking and crying. They had to stop twice and rest, even though they were walking slowly.

Jamal didn't want to stop. He wanted to be home, to be away from the dark streets. Once, he thought he saw Angel coming down the street. He stopped, his heart pounding in his chest, and pulled Tito into a doorway. It wasn't even a boy he had seen, but a girl in jeans with a yellow kerchief around her neck.

They reached Tito's house.

"I'm so scared," Tito said.

"Can you get in all right?"

"I don't know."

"Try not to cry, man," Jamal said.

"God's going to punish me," Tito said.

Jamal pulled Tito to his chest and held him. "It's gonna be all right, Tito, it's going to be all right."

"I'm going to hell," Tito said.

"They okay," Jamal said. "They just gonna be mad at us, but they okay."

"Come upstairs with me," Tito said.

Jamal didn't want to. He didn't want to be away from his house.

"Okay."

It took a long while for Tito to get the strength to walk upstairs. Jamal had to help him up the stairs. Tito opened the door, and they went in.

"Tito?" Tito's grandmother was in the bathroom, and she called to him through the door.

"Jamal's with me, Abuela," Tito said. Jamal wiped Tito's face with his hands.

They went into Tito's room, and Tito took off his clothes and got into bed.

"I got to go," Jamal said.

"Jamal, will you pray for me?"

"Yeah. You pray for me, too, okay?"

Abuela stood in the doorway. She spoke to Tito in Spanish.

"I don't feel too good," he said.

Abuela said something else in Spanish and left.

"She's going to make me some tea," Tito said.

"I got to go," Jamal said.

"Run right home," Tito said.

"Yeah."

●

Jamal was scared. Angel didn't know where he lived, but Blood and some of the other Scorpions did. They knew because they used to come around to pick up Randy sometimes. They might already be waiting for him. They could be waiting in the darkness of the hallway, or behind a parked truck. It didn't matter when they found him, but he knew they would.

Then what would he do? Angel wouldn't have a knife anymore. He would have a gun. Maybe he would be walking down his block, and they would be in the shadows. They would come out and shoot him.

He thought about the gun back at the dumpster. He thought about going to get it. He was too afraid to go back for it. He knew he was too afraid.

The streets were so dark. He started to run. He ran as fast as he could. He ran until the pain in his side slowed him and made him limp. But he didn't stop.

He went into the hallway holding his breath. Suppose they had got into his apartment? Maybe they had even got Mama and Sassy.

Jamal went up the stairs slowly, trying not to make them squeak, trying to make as little noise as possible. When he got to his floor, he went to the door quickly and unlocked it.

The house was quiet. Jamal locked the door behind him and went to Sassy's room. He put the light on. His sister was twisted in the covers, her black Cabbage Patch doll next to her.

Jamal closed the door and went to bed. Even in bed he couldn't sleep. He listened for footsteps in the hall, for strange sounds. He tried to separate the hallway noises from the street below. When he finally fell asleep, the gray light of dawn was already halfway across the living room.

●

"Jamal, I think this program is going to be just wonderful for you." Mrs. Roberts held out the pill that was supposed to make Jamal calmer in school with one hand and a small paper cup of water in the other. "I've never seen a child so hyperactive. Did you eat cereal this morning?"

"Cereal? Yeah." Jamal said.

He took the pill and the cup of water Mrs. Roberts handed him.

"That's another thing that you're going to have to cut out," Mrs. Roberts took the empty cup from Jamal and threw it in a trash can. "Most of that cereal is just loaded with sugar."

Jamal had told Mama that the pills were vitamins and that all the older kids were taking them. Mama finally signed the paper but said she would look into it later.

He wasn't sure if it was the pill or if he was just tired, but he was really okay all day. Sometimes it was almost as if he was going to fall asleep, but he didn't. Even when Billy Ware came up to him with a lot of nonsense about how he thought that Jamal could beat Dwayne, it just didn't matter.

"You say the same thing to Dwayne?" Jamal asked.

Billy stammered and looked around, and Jamal figured that he had said the same things to both of them. He laughed at Billy and then, in the middle of the laugh, forgot what he was laughing at.

There was nothing he wanted to think about and only one thing he could.

Tito hadn't come to school in the morning. He came at lunchtime with a newspaper.

"There's nothing in it," Tito said.

"They don't put stuff in the newspapers about teenagers," Jamal said. "They probably okay now anyway."

"You think so?" Tito's face was still puffy around the eyes. Jamal imagined that he must have cried all night.

"Yeah. Sure."

"I told Abuela I was in a fight. She thought I was fighting you, but I told her two big boys started bothering us."

"What she say?"

"She said . . ." Tito stopped talking and turned away. Jamal tried to move around him so he could see his face, but Tito kept turning away. Jamal saw that he was really messed around.

"It's going to be okay, man," Jamal said. "I prom-ise."

"Maybe I'll come over to your house tonight," Tito said. "We can read some comics or something."

"You can't come over for a while," Jamal said. He watched a ball bounce toward him from one of the lower grades' punchball games. He scooped it up and threw it to a small girl who had her hands out, but it went over her head. The girl put her hand on her hip and stuck out her tongue at him.

"How come I can't come over?" Tito said. "You mad at me?"

"Mad at you? You saved my life, and I'm going to be mad at you?" Jamal asked. "You can't come over because my mom's so upset over Randy."

"He still in the hospital?"

"Yeah, and she still trying to get the money to get him out," Jamal said. "Maybe next week."

Jamal didn't want to say that he was scared of the Scorpions. If they came by his house and got him, at least they wouldn't get Tito. He could see that Tito wasn't happy with his answer, but for the time being, Jamal knew it was the best he could do.

•

"So how he going back if he still all bandaged up?" Sassy asked.

"They got a hospital right in the jail," Mama said. "They say they might let him work there for six months or so, until he get his strength back."

"What the lawyer say?"

"When I couldn't get the money from Mr. Stanton, he said there wasn't too much he could do. He filed a paper asking for a transfer down to Rahway, which would make it a lot easier to go see him, but that's all."

"How about the appeal?" Jamal asked.

"Jamal, is something wrong with you?"

"No, ma'am."

"I think he been drinking," Sassy said.

"Jamal, if something's bothering you . . ."

"I'm okay," Jamal said. He managed a smile.

Mama breathed out hard. "I got to get you children out of here into someplace better. I just got to, before you and Sassy going to be in trouble too."

"I ain't going to be in no trouble," Sassy said. "I got sense."

"We all born with sense," Mama said. "Lord knows what happens to it along the way."

"You going to see Randy today?" Sassy asked.

Mama shook her head no.

After dinner Jamal put the television on and watched the news.

CHAPTER NINETEEN

"Jamal, get your clothes on so we can go to church tonight," Mama said.

"You ain't going to see Randy tonight?" Sassy asked.

"No, I just can't make it," Mama said.

"I don't feel so good," Jamal said. "I thought maybe I'd stay home."

"I've seen you acting kind of droopy this week," Mama said. "You ain't using that dope, are you?"

"Now how I look using some kind of dope?"

"Randy sat in a chair just like that one and said the same thing to me," Mama said. "And to look at his face when he was saying it, you wouldn't think butter would melt in his mouth."

"Mama, I ain't—"

"Jamal!"

"I'm going to church, Mama."

Jamal changed into his school pants, and Sassy started combing her hair. Mama put grease on Sassy's face and fixed her ribbon. It was good having Mama home in the evening. She had been making the long bus ride back and forth to Stormville every night.

He wondered how Randy would feel when she

didn't come. Would he be afraid the same way that Jamal was afraid? Maybe he would even be more afraid, thinking about going back to the regular prison, where the guys who stabbed him were.

"Jamal, Mama said don't take all day with your little ugly self," Sassy called through the bathroom door.

"I'm going to ugly you in your mouth!" Jamal called to his sister.

Jamal thought about Randy being scared up in the prison and him being scared down here in Harlem. For a while he hadn't been scared. When he had had the gun in the storeroom, he hadn't been scared. Even when they had gone to the crack house looking for Mack, he hadn't been scared. Maybe, he thought, you got messed up easily when you had a gun, but at least you weren't scared.

"Jamal!"

The super had mopped the halls down with ammonia again, the way he did once a week. The ammonia made Jamal want to throw up.

"We going to start going to church more as a family," Mama said. "And it ain't going to do you a bit of harm, so don't try to get out of it, Jamal."

"I didn't say nothing," Jamal said.

"I thought I heard him getting ready to say something, Mama."

"Sassy, how you going to tell a lie on the way to church, girl?" Mama said.

"She always got something to say," Jamal said.

Mack.

Jamal's stomach clenched when he saw him sitting on the stoop.

"Hey, I forgot what apartment you live in," Mack said. "How you doing, Mrs. Hicks?"

"I'm doing quite well," Mama said coolly.

"How Randy?"

"He's getting better," she said.

"Yo, Jamal, you got a minute?"

"I'll be at the church in a minute, Mama," Jamal said.

Mama's eyes looked fierce. "Jamal, you want to talk to this boy?"

"Yes, ma'am."

"I expect you in church in five minutes, and if I don't see you, I'm coming to get you! You understand that?"

Mama took Sassy's hand and went on down the street toward Bethel Tabernacle.

"What's up?" Jamal could smell the wine on Mack's breath. He looked around to see if any of the other Scorpions were there.

"I had to do it, man," Mack said.

"Do what?"

"I wasted Angel and Indian."

"You what?" Jamal's legs nearly gave way, and he sat down on the bannister.

"They kept messing with me, so I called for a meeting," Mack went on. "We met over at the clubhouse, and then we went for a walk and I tried to explain that I ain't the kind of dude who like to be messed with. Then they made they play, and I had to burn 'em."

"What you do?"

"We was in that little park off Lenox Avenue, you dig?"

"Marcus Garvey?"

"Yeah." Mack nodded. "When Angel made his play, I snuffed him first. Put me a hole in his head. Then Indian tried to jump into it, and I shot him, too."

"They dead?" Jamal felt his hand trembling and put it under his thigh so Mack wouldn't see it.

"Angel, he dead, but Indian got down to Joint Diseases 'mergency room. They patched him up a little and then busted him for possession. He gonna do some heavy time."

"He in the slam now?"

"Yeah, but guess what he try to pull down?"

"What?"

"He said you set him up. He said it was you and me. You was talking to him, and then I come out from behind a tree and popped him. But it don't mean nothing, because I took care of business, and now you and me, man, we the top dudes in the Scorpions. Them colors don't belong to nobody but us."

Jamal looked around. He was trying to catch his breath. "I can't carry it, man," Jamal said.

"You can carry it, little bro'."

"No, you got more heart than me," Jamal said. "Indian ain't gonna mess with you."

"Hey, you know the Mack take care of business."

"What the other Scorpions saying?"

"They layin' low," Mack said. "You waste a couple of guys, and they know who you are. You a stone killer, and they know you mean what you say."

"You got to run the Scorpions," Jamal said. "You the man, Mack."

"Yeah, maybe you right," Mack said. "'Cause you kind of young. Dudes like Indian and Blood too old for you."

"How bad Indian hurt?"

"He hurt bad, 'cause I plugged him in the neck, but he know he can't turn me because I know too many people in the joint. So all he can do is blow wind."

"You ain't going to get in trouble?"

"No, man, you don't get in no trouble you snuff somebody ain't got nothing," Mack said.

"The dealers gonna deal with you? What they say?"

"What they gonna say? They need some legs, and the Scorpions the best on the scene," Mack said. "Randy in the slam, now Indian in the slam. Angel he down there in the city icebox. You got to deal with what's on the street."

"Look, I'm gonna tell my moms to let Randy know you taking over the Scorpions. I think he gonna dig that."

"Yeah, yeah. Randy my main man. Look, I got to slide crosstown," Mack said. "I just wanted to like—you know, pull your coat to what went down."

"You think Indian gonna try to make trouble for me?"

"No, man, what he going to make trouble for you for? The deal went down the way the deal went down! You on the street, you got to take what the street put down. Yo, here comes your mama. You got to be nice to your mama, 'cause when she gone, it's a hurting thing."

"Yeah, I'll check you out later."

"And don't forget to have your moms tell Randy about me taking over the Scorpions," Mack said.

"Yeah."

Jamal watched Mack bob and dip halfway down the street, then stop and head toward the stoop.

"Yo, Jamal, I don't want you to worry about nothing, because the Scorpions is always going be in your corner, and you can check that out for the stone truth."

Mack put his hand down by his knee, palm up, and Jamal gave him five.

"What he want?" Mama asked.

"He said he taking over the Scorpions," Jamal said. "I think that's what Randy wanted him to do."

CHAPTER TWENTY

The Scorpions wore their colors to Angel's funeral. Mack had taken over, but there was talk that Blood was starting some mess. Mack said it didn't mean anything, because Blood didn't want to mess with him.

The funeral wasn't too big. There were four cars— an old, dark green Cadillac, that lined up behind the hearse, which Angel's family rode in, and two new Lincolns that the dealers had lent the Scorpions. All the kids on the block were saying how cool it was when the Scorpions busted out of the funeral parlor and into the cars.

"I'm a Scorpion, you know." A light-skinned kid, his hair in corn rows, talked with a toothpick dangling from his mouth.

Tito stayed on Jamal's mind. It was Indian who was in jail and Angel who had been killed, but Jamal knew that Tito was messed up, too. It was as if he had been wounded in a place that Jamal couldn't see, though he knew the wound was there. The week before Angel's funeral Tito wouldn't come out of his house. Jamal went over and found him sitting in his room with the shades down. He told him what

had happened, that Mack was going around saying
that it was he who had shot Angel and Indian.

"He's got him a whole story going," Jamal said.
"Like he a big man or something."

Tito whispered something that Jamal didn't hear.
Jamal turned the radio down and asked him what
he had said.

"I didn't want to kill nobody," he said.

"I know that, man." Jamal put his arm around
Tito.

Abuela wouldn't let Jamal in the next time.

"He's sick" was all she would say.

Jamal called Tito twice, but Abuela wouldn't let
him come to the phone. "Don't call," she said. "He's
too sick."

Jamal asked Mrs. Rose in the school office if she
had heard anything and she said no, she hadn't, but
that if he didn't show up soon he was going to be
left back.

After the funeral Jamal started sitting on Tito's
stoop. No matter how cold it was, he would sit on
the stoop. Sometimes Abuela would come out to go
to the store, and she would see him. He didn't say
anything to Abuela, although sometimes he thought
she wanted to say something to him.

Mama was worried about him, he knew. She kept
asking him questions about whether he was using
drugs, and once she searched the couch.

"How would you like to go down to North Carolina for the rest of the school year?" she asked him.

"I ain't going to North Carolina," Jamal had answered.

•

The Wednesday before the end of the marking period was cold, but the sun was shining. When Mr. Hunter asked Jamal for his homework and he hadn't done it, he was sent to Mr. Davidson's office right away. It was as if they were waiting for him to do something. Mr. Davidson told him that he was recommending that he be transferred to a school for problem kids.

"Okay with me," Jamal had said.

Mrs. Rich, when she found out what Mr. Davidson had said, spoke to Jamal in the hall. She told him that he didn't have to go to the other school if he didn't want to. He could leave school for the rest of the term and come back the next term.

"You'll have to do the year over again if you do that," she said. "But you might think about it. You're kind of small, and those problem children can be quite rough."

Jamal shrugged. He was glad for the way she had talked to him, like she was really interested. He didn't say it to her, but he was glad.

The next day he didn't go to school at all. He was sitting on the Tito's stoop, still thinking about what Mrs. Rich had said, thinking about how much he could make carrying packages from the A&P, when Tito came out.

He had lost weight. He looked pale as he stood

211

against the front door to his apartment building.

Jamal looked at him, started to stand, and sat back down. Tito looked as if he might run away any moment.

They stayed on the stoop for a while without speaking, and then Tito came down the stairs and started walking. Jamal got up and walked next to him.

"How you doing?" Jamal asked.

"Not too good."

"Everything's going to be okay, man," Jamal said. "Really."

"Abuela thought you beat me up," he said.

"You didn't tell her anything?"

"Jamal." Tito's voice dropped. "It's too big inside me. I had to tell her. I was getting to be sick all the time holding it in me."

"I think you gonna be okay," Jamal said. "Maybe it take some time, but you gonna be okay."

"Abuela paid a lawyer and we went to the police station," Tito said.

Jamal stopped. "What happened?"

"I told them I found a gun and that I went walking through the park, and Indian and . . . the other guy, they jumped on me." Tito turned away. "Then they asked me a whole lot of questions about if I knew anything about crack dealers and I said no. I told them I was alone. I didn't think they cared too much."

"You got to have a trial?"

"Unh-uh. They called the school to make sure how old I was, and they charged me with being a juvenile delinquent."

Jamal looked at Tito. He saw the tears running down his face, and the eyes, which suddenly looked like Abuela's.

"Tito . . ." Jamal searched for the words and couldn't find them.

"They said since I wasn't so old, I could go to Puerto Rico and stay there with my father and then I wouldn't be in trouble."

"You got to leave?"

"I wished they had beat me up," Tito said. He was crying harder now, his whole body shaking. For a long moment the two boys looked at each other without speaking.

"Tito, I'm sorry," Jamal said finally.

"Me too," Tito said. He turned away and ran into the building.

Jamal walked home slowly. There were other things he had wanted to say to Tito. He had wanted to say something about being sorry about the gun, about not throwing it away when Tito had said they should. But he hadn't been able to bring the words to his mouth. They had lain in the bottom of his stomach like rocks weighing his whole life down.

Every thought he had about the gun was bad. It had made so much trouble, had hurt them so much. But there was something else, too. Something deep in him that he thought Tito knew about, had maybe

213

known about even before he did. That was the part of him, a part that was small and afraid, that still wanted the gun.

Abuela called the day they were leaving for Puerto Rico. Mama answered the phone and spoke to her.

"Why didn't you tell me Tito was going to Puerto Rico?" Mama asked. "It's no wonder you acting so down all the time. Lord knows it ain't easy losing a friend."

"When he going to Puerto Rico?" Sassy asked.

"She say they fixing to go now," Mama said. "You want me to go over there with you to say good-bye, Jamal?"

Jamal said no.

He got the drawing he had been working on of Tito. It was the best drawing he had done in his whole life. He rolled it up and wrapped it carefully in plastic wrap.

"You okay, Jamal?" Sassy asked.

Jamal nodded.

"It's a real good picture," Sassy said. "He's going to like it."

It was Sunday afternoon, and Tito's block was crowded with people. Some men were playing touch football in the street. Abuela and Tito were already in front of the house, their bags on the sidewalk, when Jamal got there. Tito turned away when Jamal got to him, and Jamal thought that he was mad. He stepped around him to look into his face and saw that Tito was crying again.

"I get me a boat I'm coming to Puerto Rico to see you," Jamal said.

Tito smiled, and the tears in his eyes sparkled.

"You look ugly when you cry," Jamal said.

"Everybody looks ugly when they cry," Tito said.

A taxi, its fenders rusted and its company name painted on the door, pulled up to the curb. Abuela started putting their bags in the backseat.

"You want to take this with you?" Jamal took his drawing out of the plastic wrap.

Tito looked at the picture. Then he looked at Jamal. "I don't look like this no more," he said. "I look different now."

He handed the drawing back to Jamal and ran to the cab.

Jamal stood, his back against the red brick of the Harlem tenement. He watched as the short, stocky driver finished putting the last bag into the battered cab.

The cab pulled away from the curb. Jamal turned down the block and began walking home. He didn't think—almost didn't feel, except for the stinging in his eyes, a dull pain in his throat that was there and not there at the same time. He walked on, with the wind in his face and the sounds of a blues record crackling over a cheap loudspeaker as he passed the vegetable store.

"Jamal!"

At first he didn't think he had really heard his name over the sounds of the street. He thought it might have been just the wind blowing across the flapping tin signs of the abandoned stores, or the distant wailing of some kid's boom box.

"Jamal!"

He turned and there was the cab, moving slowly along the street. It stopped, and the door opened and Tito came rushing out. Tito came to him and grabbed him and hugged him and kissed him on his face.

Tito stood and looked for a moment at his friend, then took the picture from him. Their eyes met.

"Tito." Abuela's voice.

In a moment that passed so quickly that it was almost a memory before it happened, Tito had turned and run back to the cab.

There was a dark figure in the back window of the cab as it pulled away. Jamal couldn't tell if it was Abuela or Tito as he waved.

The wind picked up. It was colder, much colder than it had been. A tall kid in sneakers, walking in the same direction that Jamal was, looked him over. Jamal tilted his head back and hardened his stare. The kid looked away. Jamal pulled his collar up against the wind.

WALTER DEAN MYERS

has written many books for young adults. His first
book, FAST SAM, COOL CLYDE, AND STUFF, published in
1975, was an ALA Notable. He was twice recipient
of the Coretta Scott King Award, and his books have
received many awards and honors. Mr. Myers and
his family live in New Jersey.